Foster to Family

Famous in a Small Town

Book 1

M.L. Pennock

Also by M.L. Pennock

To Have — Brian and Stella's story
To Hold (To Have #2) — Stephanie and Max's story
To Cherish (To Have #3) — Tommy and Jacelyn's story
Letters from Emily (To Have #4)

Coming soon ...

The Bakery on Main (Famous in a Small Town, Book 2)

Dedication

This book is dedicated to the families who have opened their hearts and homes to the countless number of children in foster care throughout America.

To learn more about foster care, visit the following organizations on the web:

U.S. Department of Health and Human Services

Child Welfare Information Gateway

AdoptUSKids

Table of Contents

Chapter 1

MAY
Delilah

So, here's the thing. I have deep adoration and admiration for people who can decide to do something and then just do it. I have loads of respect for them. It's like they wake up one day, hell bent on being the next whoever is the best in their field, and they just dive in head first and make it happen.

That is not me. I have to ponder and wonder and obsess slightly about what's going to work and what isn't. I'm a trained pastry chef, I specialize in wedding cakes and confections, and I've spent the last eight years of my life working in grocery store bakeries. In my spare time I make specialty cupcakes and cakes and whatnot, but the daily grind is me hidden away decorating cartoon character birthday cakes for children who maybe aren't even going to remember in five years they liked that show.

I am not living my best life. What I am doing is settling for comfort because trying something new is scary. I'm sure you've felt that way a time or two, right? I can't even bring myself to charge for the sweets I bake on a specialty basis because it's always for friends and family. They pay me with love and coffeehouse gift cards and the occasional fifty slipped under the flower vase on the table in my living room.

"Lilah, you almost done with those cupcakes? Mrs. Stratford is here to pick them up," Maggie asks from the door.

"Uh, yes?" I look down at the four dozen mini vanilla cupcakes that still need to be frosted. Stella ordered twelve dozen of them for a teacher appreciation gift at the elementary school — six with blue frosting and the rest are white. Thankfully, I just need to finish the white ones. I start moving my arm, swirling the buttercream on as quickly as I can and say, "I should be done in twenty."

Maggie chuckles and shakes her head as she pushes back through the door. She's muffled, but I hear nothing more than her joyful, vibrant voice making me believe there are no issues with me running behind.

Fifteen minutes later I'm putting the final swirl on the last cupcake and closing the clamshell container as my phone buzzes in my pocket — the alarm I set for myself. I beat the clock. Stacking the containers one on top of another, I carry four at a time out to the bakery counter and look around for Stella before going in for the last set of cupcakes.

I see her as I push back through the door, arms loaded with blue frosted cupcakes, and smile.

"Sorry I held you up. I didn't realize I was that far behind when you came in earlier. You'll have time to get these to the school still?"

"I've got plenty of time. Lunches start in about a half hour, so I'll get there and finish setting up as the classes dismiss to eat. It was a huge order, though. I should have given you more notice than two days," she says.

"I'm still confused why you come here instead of just having your husband make them at the coffee shop."

Stella rolls her eyes and says, "Don't even get me started about the bureaucratic red tape of the PTO."

"That bad, huh?" I ask, wrinkling my nose.

"You can only imagine. However, their insistence that the baked goods come from the grocery store means I get to see my favorite pastry queen," she says, biting her lip as she finishes. I wait patiently for her to tell me what else she needs. "There's this party I'm planning. It's kind of a big deal."

I smile and my eyes go wide, as I say, "Oh really?"

"It's my parents' anniversary next month. Would you be willing to take it on? Cake, cupcakes, some fancy cookies, the whole nine yards?"

Trust me when I say I love small orders. It gives me a chance to really pay attention to the details for each piece. But ...

All my years of stalling, of standing right where I am because I'm comfortable, shake on their already unsteady foundation. It's been really rickety for a while now, and the more I get lost in my own fantasies while trying to do my job tells me I'm on extremely shaky ground. All it might take to bring me out of complacency is one solid offer like what Stella's presenting now. I smile despite the immense fear of failure that's crawling up the back of my neck and take a deep breath.

"I ... I would love to," I say. Stella's eyes light up with pure joy. "Can you get me a color scheme and some ideas of what you're looking for by the weekend? I'll get some samples together and we can schedule a time to meet next week."

"That would be wonderful. Here's my cell number and the house phone number," she says, handing me a business card with all her information on it. "And my email is on there, too, just in case."

As she finishes loading her cupcakes in the grocery cart beside her, I reach across the counter to shake her hand and effectively seal the deal.

"I'm so excited you said yes. I was afraid you would have too much going on to be able to take on one more thing. I'll be in touch with the details," Stella says. She smiles once more before turning away with her order and heading to the checkout line.

I busy myself with wiping down the counter and then head back into the kitchen area to clean up the frosting mess from the marathon cupcake decorating. My mind wanders to the different recipes I'd like to try for Stella's parents' event and as morning slowly creeps by, I continuously have to pull my thoughts back from all the plans filtering through my head. It's not an easy task, though, as I've baked and frosted everything that needs to be baked and frosted for the day. Maggie left shortly after the lunch hour, which is just one more reason I'm hunched over the counter with a pencil firmly grasped in my hand ignoring the regular goings on of the store. The piece of loose-leaf paper in front of me is filled with doodles — mostly icing designs for cookies and a tiered cake — for upcoming projects and, of course, the beginnings of the goodies I'd like to make for Stella's parents. When the afternoon crew comes in, I make my exit quickly without exchanging more words than I need to.

Grabbing my purse from the breakroom, I head straight for the baking aisle with a basket and promptly fill it with the ingredients I know I'm running low on at home.

"Don't you get enough baking when you're here, Delilah?" asks Mike, one of the managers, as he scans my items. "I know you've got all the fancy training and whatever, but I can't imagine liking something enough to do it full-time at a job and then go home and do more of it."

I smile as though I haven't heard this from him a hundred times before. He's nearly in his forties and this is the only job he's ever known. Granted, he's gone from stocking shelves as a job in high school, to being a cashier, to now being a manager, so he's moved up the food chain a bit over his couple of decades with the company. But, he doesn't love it. This isn't his dream and that's why he doesn't understand how I can do something here for eight hours and then go home and do it for another six just for the joy of it and the pleasure it brings to those around me.

"What can I say, Mike? I just really love what I do. If I didn't enjoy it, I don't think I would continue doing it," I say, smiling broadly at him. "Besides, you don't complain about my extracurricular baking when I make those macarons you adore."

His cheeks turn a slight shade of pink as he responds, "Well, you've got me there."

I hand him the money to cover my bill and reach for my bags as he cashes me out.

"Have a good day, Mike," I say as he hands me my receipt and change.

He smiles and nods, saying, "You as well," before I walk away.

*****

My apartment is just a few blocks from work. On nice days like today, I enjoy the walk even while carrying groceries and my purse. The breeze keeps me from breaking out in too much of a sweat, but by the time I get to the apartment, I'm ready to turn on the air conditioner and strip out of my work clothes. I walk in the door, kick my shoes off, and put the bags on a small café table in the corner. I slip my shirt off as I adjust the thermostat and then head for the bedroom, shedding my pants and tossing them in the hamper once there. Turning to my closet I pull one of my favorite dresses from its hanger, pull it up my legs, and slide the zipper up the small of my back.

I love dresses. They're classic. Some people think I'm stuck in the 1950s, but really I just love how comfortable they are. Plus, if ever I find the right guy, they offer easy access ... not that I'm looking for a guy. I have too much going on with work. A brief feeling of sadness climbs into my chest before I smile at myself in the mirror and choose not to acknowledge the loneliness.

Cakes. Cupcakes. Cookies. Fondant. Frosting. Those are my loves. Ain't nobody got time for emotional attachments to people when there are so many things to bake. I grab my phone and earbuds, plugging them in as I walk through the living room in my postage stamp sized one-bedroom apartment, and soon my ears are filled with Jimi Hendrix as he helps me get out of my own head and into the kitchen where I belong, where I feel the most at home.

Bowls begin to fill with ingredients. The stand mixer whirs to life as I prepare batter for vanilla bean cupcakes and a small tasting cake. The mixer folds the batter while I carefully measure into another dish the confectioner's sugar and butter for the buttercream. Wild orange would be delicious with the vanilla, I decide, and pull out my collection of jars filled with magic flavors. I get lost in Jimi's voice as I work my kitchen witchery and only stop briefly to pile my ginger hair on top of my head, securing it with a heavy-duty elastic band.

The oven beeps, telling me it's up to temperature, as I finish filling the cupcake papers and cake pan. Soon, my entire apartment will smell like heaven. I imagine heaven smells like a bakery, because why wouldn't it? People don't say, "It smells heavenly in here," when they walk into a patisserie for no reason. The saying had to have come from somewhere. I choose to believe it was information provided to a select few in the beginning by the angels themselves. Heaven smells like fresh baked cakes and powdered sugar.

Once everything is in the oven, I whip up the buttercream and pull fondant out that I already have on hand. Flowers are done so frequently on cakes for weddings and anniversaries, but they're also a standard. I just don't want to do roses. Everyone does roses. Stargazer lilies. Dahlias. Morning glories. Those aren't common. I opt for stargazers along the side of the cake and roll out the fondant to begin cutting to shape.

I won't lie. I'm tired from already working all day. But, as I give myself over to creating little masterpieces in my tiny kitchen, the tired doesn't matter much. When the cupcakes are cooled and the cake is sprung free from its pan, I breathe out a sigh of relief that they're baked to perfection before beginning the decorating process. This is my favorite part, despite my back starting to ache from standing.

From what I've noticed through my interactions with her, Stella can be a perfectionist. It doesn't matter these are just tasting cakes and not the final version of what I'll make for her parents' anniversary gathering. I really want them to be the best representation of what I can offer their guests. I snap pictures with my phone of the process and, when all the decorating is done and I've had time to wrap my head around pricing, I'll send them to her so she can see the ideas I've come up with.

When I started playing in the kitchen after work today, I made sure to cover the clocks. Sounds weird, I know. Unless I have the timer set to pull things from the oven, the last thing I want distracting me is a damn clock. So, I stick a Post-It over the microwave and oven clocks and, well, I just never bothered to put up a wall clock when I moved in. I have a method to my madness. Immersion. Who really wants to be a clock watcher when creating magic? Not me. No thanks. As you can imagine, this can be problematic as well, and I frown as I tug the sticky note from the oven and see it's well past midnight.

"Shit." I scrub my hands down my face and quickly begin clearing the counters of the mess I've left behind. Glancing at the day's confections, I smile and feel a sense of pride lift within me. "At least these cakes look fucking phenomenal."

Before I cover the baked goods for the night, I pull my phone out again and snap a few more pictures. I cannot wait to start my little business.

Chapter 2

Fisher

When I first started working at my parents' restaurant, this was the last thing I wanted to do for the rest of my life. But I loved my mom and dad, and my little sister and me helping out was important to them. If they were still here, I'm not sure my life would be much different than it is now, with the exception that I might get a day off here and there.

I was a C student at the local community college when my parents were killed in a car accident. At the time, Jacelyn was off living her dreams in California, doing the university thing and working on her degree in fine arts. She was home for the holidays and in seconds our lives changed. One phone call from the police. One trip to Rochester on a snowy night. One deep breath before realizing nothing would ever be the same again.

That's all it took. That's how Jacelyn and I became owners of my parents' restaurant, Canalside Grill. It was thrust upon us and, though we wouldn't have it any other way and we never would have sold or closed the restaurant at that point, we were forced to grow up quickly.

No, that's not entirely true. I was the one who was forced to grow up quickly. I'm not saying she didn't have to mature overnight when Mom and Dad died, but I made sure she went back to California and focused on that degree she wanted. Jace finished school and has a white picket fence life. It was her lifelong goal to be a well-known artist and she has that along with so much more, even if she's only "well-known" in our community.

I, on the other hand, dropped out to run the restaurant full time and lied to my sister on a monthly basis about how well things were going. That's just the way it was. I didn't want her to worry. Truth is, I didn't want her to see me messing up and come home to fix it.

That was literally years ago, though, and we're in much better places now. For instance, she moved back home to Brockport, married the guy who helped me turn the business around, and lives minutes from me. They also made me an uncle, so, you know, that's amazing. As for me, the restaurant is booming. I'm successful.

No. We are successful.

I've been doing this so long now I can't imagine doing anything else. Sometimes I do think about what more I could do with this business though. Through conversations with Jacelyn and Tommy, I've quietly played with the idea of expanding into catering. There have been enough people in the past asking about supplying food for small parties and business events that we would be stupid to not take it into consideration.

Sitting at the raised counter in my sister's kitchen with a cup of coffee in one hand and a pen in the other, I catch her staring at me. I give her a look, lifting one eyebrow as if to question her.

"You're sighing."

"I'm sighing?"

"You're loud about it."

"Is sighing not allowed?"

She smiles. "It is, unless it's from you. You don't sigh unless there's something heavy on your mind. Out with it."

This time I notice when I make the sound she's referred to and I groan, dropping my head back to look at the ceiling.

"Would it be stupid to expand the business?"

When she says nothing, I lift my head. She blinks, but doesn't say anything.

"We're in a good spot financially, we're busier than we've ever been, and people love our food," I say. She takes a sip of her coffee and nods. I continue. "Would you be opposed to me taking us to the next level and offering catering services?"

I don't know why I'm nervous to ask her. She's always been supportive. Jace has been my backbone when I forget there's more to me than our parents' legacy. Catering is a big leap though, and I don't want to make it exclusive to small functions. There are plenty of other restaurants offering these things and we need to stand out. I've never been an attention seeker. This is difficult. Being the face of a business isn't something I have ever gotten used to because behind the scenes is where the fun happens.

I feel infinitely calmer when she reaches her hand out and grasps my wrist to stop me from tapping the pen against the table. She smiles at me instead of responding first. She listens while reserving judgment and waits to say anything until she's sure I'm done speaking.

"I don't know, Fish. Do we have the staff for that?" she questions, a smirk playing at the edge of her mouth.

"How long have you waited for me to do this?" I ask.

She stands and walks toward the refrigerator, opens the door, and pulls out a container of yogurt. She's quiet and contemplative as she returns to the table after pulling a spoon from the drawer beside the sink.

"Since I was working the bar and noticed how many larger groups were trying to book us on a regular basis."

I stare at her incredulously. She hasn't consistently helped me out in the bar in at least a year.

"I didn't say anything because I knew you were trying to get a handle on the business doing more than staying afloat. Plus, with trying to open the art gallery and paint shop, I knew I wasn't going to have the extra time to take on catering, too. Then, I was pregnant and married and life happens," she says. "But, I think this is a great idea and I'm all in if you need us."

"Us? Are you offering Tommy up as tribute?" I laugh.

"I am. We love you and want the family businesses to succeed. Considering the help you've given me with my business and Tommy with his, and of course Brian and Greg at the coffeehouse, do you really think we wouldn't return the favor?"

The thing is, I've asked for so many favors in the past. What happens when they get tired of helping me? Instead, I ask her when she could have possibly talked to him about something like this since it's the first time we've ever discussed it.

She takes a bite of her yogurt, swallows, and then gives me a look. I don't even know this look. I haven't seen it before. Not on her at least ... but on Mom? Yes. And that hits me hard in the center of my chest.

"It's been a discussion because we know how your brain works."

"You looked like Mom just now," I blurt out, and her face softens more.

"I love you, too. Now, when are we going to figure out menus and prices?"

*****

Stuffed shells. Twice baked potatoes. Chicken three different ways. Portobello mushrooms. Prime rib. Grilled asparagus. Baked pears with caramel glaze. Red wine. White wine. Tea. Coffee. Jacey's Mexican Hot Chocolate cinnamon rolls. Cheesecake. Scones.

The list of things I want on this menu is endless and in the few days I've been trying to put it all together, people have found out the plan. It's not even a plan yet. It's just an idea with a list of food right now.

That hasn't stopped us from getting phone calls asking for consultations. Even when I tell the people contacting me I don't have a complete menu or a price list, they brush it off and ask for my availability anyway.

"I might be in over my head," I say to Tommy as he types away while sitting at the bar. The food list is in front of me. It's a mess. "I have no organizational skills."

He glances over at my paper and then back at his screen. "Make columns according to the menu item. Appetizers. Entrees. Sides. Desserts. Drinks. At the top of each column, put your price point. You're making it harder than it needs to be." He turns his computer around so I can see what he's been working on. "How's this look?"

My assumption that he had been working on a marketing project for a client goes out the window as I stare at the breakdown of a catering contract and the beginnings of the menu layout.

"It's not even close to done, but it's a start. I need the digital files of the restaurant logo, unless you're thinking of rebranding for the catering side of things and need a new design."

"That looks amazing. Should we do a new logo for the catering? I don't even know where to begin with that. Am I using a different name? Is it all the same business? Tommy, help me," I plead.

He takes a sip of his beer.

"What's Jacelyn say? Talk to her about it. I know you're all about the family and keeping in line with what your parents wanted for this place," he says. I hear the "but" without him saying it. "However, the catering is a hundred percent you and your sister. Maybe you should come up with a new business name specifically for it. Create a logo and marketing plan that fits this new adventure."

I nod. He has valid points.

"Maybe she'll design something for us," I think out loud, tapping my pen against the bar.

"I'll be surprised if she hasn't already started. This is all she's talked about for days," Tommy says without looking up from his computer.

I slip the pen behind my ear and pull my phone from my pocket. Bringing up the last message from Jace, I send her a quick note. All it says is, "Show me what you've got?"

Within minutes, she's sent me photos of several designs. The last message to come through is a text.

Jace: I assume this is what you meant by that?

I snicker.

Me: Yeah I did. Any one in particular you like more than the others?

I wait a few more minutes, scrolling back over the photos. Each design is more intricate than the last.

Jace: The last one, but I think we should put them side-by-side and look at them together.

Me: Coffee. Tomorrow. Your house.

Jace: Coffee. Tomorrow. The Bean. I need to be in the studio most of the day. Kathryn is keeping the baby.

Me: Game on.

"Told you so. What time tomorrow?"

"What are you? Psychic?" I question.

He holds his phone up and I see a notification from Jacey. Impulsively, I roll my eyes.

"No set time, just said she's in the studio tomorrow, your mama is keeping the baby, and to meet at the Bean."

Closing his laptop and sliding it into the case, Tommy smiles. "Awesome. See you at seven, then."

"But! That's so early." I'm used to sleeping a little later since I don't have to be at the restaurant until at least nine in the morning. We don't do breakfast, so I get in midmorning to get lunch rolling.

He turns and begins making his way to the kitchen to leave through the back entrance. "Not nearly as early as it could be. She's usually up by five to try to get a jumpstart to the day before Jonah wakes up. She's a fucking machine lately trying to do everything. I would try to be early if I were you."

He doesn't even wait for me to respond. I suppose I should feel lucky Jacelyn didn't tell me to come to the house first thing in the morning. I'm not sure I could handle my sister any earlier than seven.

*****

I stroll in through the back of the coffeehouse just before seven the next morning. The fact I arrived on the scene with my own coffee in hand should tell you something.

"Not a morning person, eh?" Greg says as I make my way through the kitchen.

"No, not really. Is Jacey here yet? I'm supposed to be meeting her to go over some ideas for the restaurant."

He nods and points to the café door separating the kitchen from the rest of the coffeehouse.

"She came through about five minutes before you did muttering something about the baby not sleeping well," he says while tossing sugar in the mixer.

I drop my head back and look at the ceiling.

"She's going to be grumpy with me. What if I just sneak back out the door and you tell her I forgot my phone at home and we'll get together later?"

"No, sir. I am not getting in the middle of anything going on with you and your sister. That's Tommy's job. Besides, you're trying to get a new business off the ground and she's there to help you. We're all here to help you, Fisher. Just, get your ass out there and tame the beast. Take her a chocolate chocolate chip muffin and be the best big brother you can be," Greg says. "And then offer to babysit tonight so she can go to bed early."

Grabbing a muffin off the cooling rack and a plate from the cupboard, I steel myself for this meeting with my baby sister. The baby sister who has more world experience in her pinky than I have in my whole body. The little kid I used to throw flour at during family baking nights when we were barely teenagers. The girl who taught me how strong I needed to be so she didn't need to be strong for both of us.

"Fine. But if this goes south, I'm coming to you for backup."

My sister terrifies me in the best ways.

I adjust the strap for my messenger bag, take a deep breath, and back myself through the door.

"Good luck, Fish," Greg says. He salutes me as if I'm heading off to battle, but smiles because he knows Jacey and I don't fight. Not like normal families might. Our disagreements are solidly built on our love for one another because we've only had each other for so long. "I'll come check on you in a few."

Nodding, I push the rest of the way through the door and turn to find my sister standing at the counter. I wait a beat, watching her hover over her planner with a cell phone in one hand and a pen in the other.

Clearing my throat, I break her concentration. "Do you already have a table?"

She looks up, eyes glazed over from exhaustion, and points toward the front windows. "Near the sun."

The sun. Not the window. The sun.

"Got it," I say and make my way to the table she's picked. Her sketchbook and pens are scattered there along with the custom travel mug I got her for Christmas last year. Picking up the mug to see how full it is, I ask, "Do you need a refill, Jace?"

"Always," she says, coming up behind me. "Take the top off. I snagged the pot Greg just made."

"Thief. Don't you know you don't work here?"

She laughs, but we both know how our family businesses run. We help ourselves to the coffee and toss extra in the tip jar for the college kids.

"Tommy picked on me forever when we first got married because I still was afraid to go behind the counter and fill my own cup," she says.

"Have you been able to fill your cup recently?"

She finishes pouring and looks me dead in the eyes before responding.

"Helping you start this new business. That's filling my cup."

Chapter 3

Delilah

Having a day off is kind of a rare thing for me. I don't like not being busy. Lack of things to do gives me too much time to think and who needs that? But I suppose a day off to reset myself is occasionally necessary.

"Large hot cocoa for here," I say to the kid at the counter.

Stella's talked about the hot chocolate recipe they use at her husband's café, and though I'm perfectly capable of making my own from the packets in my apartment, I needed a little change of scenery.

I pass my money to the cashier and toss the change in the tip jar when he hands it back to me. He lets me know my drink will be right up, so I thank him and turn to find a place to sit. There are a few tables covered with laptops and research papers where college students are quietly doing what they do at the end of a semester and a handful of other tables with small groups deep in conversation. It's still early, so the place isn't packed like it usually is when I walk past. I rarely come in because I'm trying to save money. I was trying to save money when I moved from a two-bedroom apartment to a one-bedroom, and I regret it most minutes of the day. Stopping for drinks and muffins on a regular basis means spending what I could be putting away for baking supplies and getting back into a larger home. This one time, though, two dollars won't break me. That's what I tell myself.

I find the one table furthest away from everyone and tuck myself in the corner before pulling my notebooks and colored pencils out of the tote bag I've carried since I was eleven. I place one earbud in and leave the other hanging free before opening the music app on my phone. Ella Fitzgerald's voice fills my head as the smells of the café waft around me, wrapping me up In their warmth.

The sketchbook before me is filled with ideas from simple cupcakes to intricate, multi-tiered wedding monstrosities I've dreamed up. I turn to a clean page and close my eyes letting the images come to me before placing the tip of my pencil to the paper. The sketch takes on a life of its own and as I work quietly in the corner I hardly notice when the barista brings my cocoa over. I don't even pick it up to taste it until after it's cooled considerably. Pulling the milky chocolate across my tongue I wish I had tasted it while it was still hot as I can only assume, given how delectable it is cooled, it must have been twice as good freshly made.

Before long I notice the other people around me have left. With the exception of one couple arguing about mashed potatoes versus twice baked, I'm the only one still here.

"You're being ridiculous. Why does it have to be one or the other?" the woman scolds. "Dad would have put both on there and you know it."

"This isn't Dad's menu, though. It's ours. Do we want to give too many options? It's a catering service, not a diner," the man responds. He isn't facing me so I can't see his expression, but his voice is cold, exasperated, and I completely feel him. But, he's also kind of being a dick about it. "I want this to be fancy. People are used to coming in the restaurant and having every damn potato option possible. I want to narrow the focus."

I try — really, I do — to focus my own attention on the cake designs in front of me, but something about the way he speaks to her gets under my skin.

"You know what, Fish, you're right," the woman says. Her voice is calm. Really calm. It's the kind of calm that says she's done playing around and I smirk behind the wave of red curls falling against my cheek. "Let's narrow the focus. Do twice baked."

"But I really like mashed."

"It's not about you. I like twice baked." I see from the corner of my eye her mouth lift in a half smile as she takes a sip of her drink. "Different people have different preferences and you need to not be a potato Nazi. Offer. Both. People like choices."

The man hangs his head in defeat.

"You've made your point." He lifts his hands in surrender. "I'm sorry."

She begins to push her chair back, picking her cup up as she stands, and says, "I knew you would understand where I was coming from. I take my starches very seriously. Don't fuck with them. I need to get to the studio, but I'll send Tommy the final files for the logo today so he can get started on the letterhead." The man nods slightly. "You know this is a good move for the restaurant, right? Mom and Dad would be really proud of the direction you're taking it, Fisher."

I tuck my hair behind my ear, fully invested in a conversation that has nothing to do with me, and listen as he quietly says, "I know. I'm just afraid of messing it up."

"That is why you have me and the rest of the family here to support you. You're not doing it alone, but you are in charge and you're going to do amazing things. I'm just here to make sure you don't limit yourself too much. Today it's potatoes, tomorrow it could be putting an expansion on the back of the building but ultimately, you'll make the final decisions. The point is, big brother, I want to make sure you're making them the smart way." I bite my bottom lip as I watch her check her watch, wishing I could understand what it feels like to love a sibling that much. When she lifts her eyes from her wrist, she locks onto me. I quickly look away, fiddling with the vermillion-colored pencil in my hand, as my ears heat from being caught eavesdropping. "I'm off. I love you. Call me later."

His chair pushes back from the table and I hear the rustling of fabric as he hugs his sister.

"I love you, too. Have a good day in the studio."

I look up as she walks toward the front door and catch a glimpse of his face as he gathers his papers, laptop, and coffee mug. I try not to watch as he slings a messenger bag over his shoulder and heads toward the café kitchen, but can't ignore the way his slacks tightly hug his perfect ass.

*****

I've sat in this booth to the point my thighs are tingly and numb when I move my legs and my fingers hurt from the amount of drawing I've gotten done this morning.

"Are you done with this, ma'am?" the kid from the front counter asks and I jump slightly not realizing he was standing beside my table until he spoke. "Didn't mean to scare you. Would you like another hot chocolate?"

"No, thank you. It was delicious, but one is my limit," I say smiling up at him. "You didn't scare me. I was just sort of lost in thought."

I watch him glance down at the papers strewn about the table, the colored pencils and fine tip markers scattered about.

"Those are gorgeous. Are they cupcakes?"

"They are. Well, they're going to be."

"I don't know if I would be able to eat something that looks like a piece of art," he says, his cheeks pinking slightly. "Do you sell them?"

"I'm trying to. These are a special order for a friend. It's the first order I've actually put a price tag on and it's kind of nerve wracking," I say.

Why am I giving this person so much information? I don't know him.

"Well, those are going to be worth every cent and then some," he says, picking up my cup from the table. "I assume whatever you're charging probably isn't enough."

I begin gathering my supplies, feeling my focus slip.

I purse my lips and think briefly about what he just said, stopping him with a hand on his arm as he turns from the table.

"Why do you say that? That I'm probably not charging enough?"

"You said you're making them for a friend and it's the first order you're actually charging for. We all think our work is worth less than it really is when we're giving or selling it to friends and family," he says matter-of-factly. I must give him a look without realizing it because he continues explaining himself. "I'm a business student. It was a discussion in my class last week. All I'm saying is, if the final product looks anything remotely like that sketch, consider adding ten percent for people who aren't friends."

I open my mouth thinking words might come out, maybe a "thank you," but they don't and he gets called away by a man near the kitchen entrance before I can say anything at all.

Chapter 4

Fisher

"You need to find a girlfriend," Tommy says, breaking me from my thoughts. "I've never seen you go on a date or even show interest, romantically, in another human."

He's become accustomed to sitting at the bar working on his computer in the restaurant after we close a couple nights a week. We all quietly go about our business — T in front of a screen and the kitchen staff cleaning up while I restock the bar and check on all the administrative things I try not to worry about during open hours — so I'm surprised when he brings up my love life, or lack thereof.

I haven't been on a date since before my sister moved back home. Considering she's been back long enough to find a husband, have a baby, and open her own business on top of continuing to help me with the family restaurant ... let's just say it's a little depressing how single I really am. But, I don't have time to date. There's the restaurant to think about, and when I'm not tied up with business things, I'm busy with my family. It's taken me a lot of years to come back to putting family first. After our parents died, it was just me and Jacey. She was out in California, so really it was just me when she wasn't home for a couple days at Christmas each year.

The meaning of family was lost for us until she moved back and started seeing Tommy. If not for Tommy and the entire Stratford clan, and his sister-in-law's family, I don't know if Jace and I would have come back to the place we were at before Mom and Dad died. Now, it's morning coffee and Sunday brunch and not going a day without talking to someone I'm related to — either by blood or by marriage in some way.

"I'm not gay," I respond. It seems most people who take an interest in what I'm doing romantically automatically assume I like guys because I don't have a girlfriend and am somewhat aloof about it. I'm also a little extra about my grooming, so that occasionally raises an eyebrow or two.

He laughs and looks up from his laptop. Tommy picks up the bottle of beer he's been nursing for the last hour and kills it.

"I wouldn't care if you were, but I know you aren't gay. Why would you think I think you're gay? I've known you long enough," he says, rubbing his palms against his eyes. "Besides, I've seen your porn collection. There's really nothing gay about that."

I roll my eyes and toss the towel I was using to dry glasses over my shoulder.

"Spill it. Why do I need to find a girlfriend?"

"Your sister said so," he says. He gives me a crooked smile. "I promised her I would talk to you about it and make sure everything was okay."

Why wouldn't everything be okay?

"Things are fine. I'm just busy, you know? Things have really picked up here and with the fall wedding planning season in full swing, I've got a bunch of catering jobs on top of Jenny and Dale's anniversary party. I'm feeling short staffed and over worked, and when I'm not here, I'm with you guys or at home sleeping." I shrug and hope that's a good enough answer. I don't want him to get the idea to do to me what his brother, Brian, and friend, Max, did to him before he met Jacelyn. The dating website thing didn't exactly work in his favor. I saw one train wreck after another walk through here brokenhearted because he honestly had no interest.

"We noticed." He doesn't say it snidely. There's more concern in his tone than accusation of me being a third wheel. "I know how lonely being alone can get, and Jacey knows that, too. She's just worried."

"And I love her for that, but I'm fine," I smile. I even breathe out a laugh to lighten the mood. Despite all that, I still feel like I need to convince Tommy — and myself — that it's all okay the way it is. "There's no need to worry. I'll find someone eventually. I mean, you found someone, so it can't be that hard."

"Touché." He laughs and stands from the barstool. Tommy has free reign when he's here — after all, if not for him there wouldn't be a restaurant — so he walks behind the bar, drops his bottle in the case box and leans back against the cupboards. "But, in my defense, I wasn't really looking for anyone until Jacey. We just kind of fell together."

I nod. I know their history, so he doesn't need to remind me. I love their love story, even if I was scared to death he was going to break her heart and leave me to pick up the pieces. I wonder what he'd think if he knew that was some of why I'm not worried about finding someone? If he knew I was afraid of getting broken? I'm the last of all of us to be alone.

Already in my thirties and don't even have a prospect. I could be the single uncle who's a lot of fun to hang out with instead of getting all attached to someone. There's really nothing wrong with that, right?

"So, what do you propose?" I ask. "Don't say the Internet."

"God, no. I wouldn't wish that on anyone. You saw the types I ended up with," he says. Crossing his arms over his chest, he stares at me. "Nah, I think you're right. You're fine. For now. But I also think you need to stop being so blind and occasionally ask a woman out for drinks or dinner."

Dinner and drinks. I could do that. I nod as he pushes away from the counter and gathers his laptop bag.

"And take her somewhere you don't know everyone," he remarks as he walks toward the door. "No one should meet the entire family on the first date."

*****

By the time I walk through the door of my childhood home it's well past midnight. I drop my backpack and messenger bag on the butcherblock top island in the center of the room and look at my surroundings. Nothing here has changed, but everything has changed. Tommy and Jacelyn are right. I need to start dating. It's lonely here and, as much as I hate to admit it, I don't like being lonely even though I have no problem being alone. The issue is, these days I find comfort in the mundane. Routine is good and I'm not all over the place the way I was before Tommy and I started working together. He got me grounded, but now maybe I'm too grounded, too rooted in my ways. For a while I was too wild and free, and that was a detriment to the business and myself. Finding balance is not a strength I have and I push myself from one extreme to another.

Pulling a sheet of paper from the folder in my bag, I try to make a pro-con list of my datable qualities. There are more cons than not and, well, that's instantly depressing. I take a shot in the dark hoping she's left her phone downstairs or on silent, and send my sister a text asking her what my good qualities are. The conversation with T has me wondering what things other women would find honorable and attractive. My sister probably isn't the best person to ask, but she's the only one I feel really comfortable having this conversation with.

I was hoping she wouldn't respond. I should have known better.

Jace: The hell, Fisher? So many good things. You're kind, smart, have a nice smile, you have me as a sister and any woman would be fortunate to have me as their future sister-in-law, you know how to cook. I could go on. Shall I?

Ugh, she's right. I do have a nice smile. I send back a message to let her know I don't need a longer list.

Jace: Tommy talked to you, didn't he? You know I'm only trying to look out for you. The business is only one part of you. There are a lot of other parts that matter and you always forget about them.

Me: I'm aware. I just don't know how to not be like this.

Jace: I saw a girl at the coffeehouse when we met last week. You should find out who she is.

Me: Any discernible qualities so I can find this mystery woman?

*Jace: She was drawing something. *shrug* I'm sure if you ask around Greg or Brian would know who she is. Go to bed. Worry about this after you get through the anniversary party this weekend.*

Me: Yes, ma'am. Goodnight.

I wait for her "goodnight" and then plug my phone in, leaving the conversation there but only until I have a chance to give it more thought. Free time to think? That might happen by Sunday.

Chapter 5

JUNE
Delilah

The cakes are loaded into Stella's Chevy Suburban, which is enormous compared to my Jeep, but I needed the extra space for the size of the order. I don't want anything to go wrong with my first big event.

The cookies are all neatly boxed by shape, each shape with its own color scheme. I've shown the same amount of detail to the cupcake containers.

I climb into the driver's seat and take the deepest breath of my life. This is huge for me. Not a little huge like when she asked me to take this order, but huge huge because I've actually completed it and am about to deliver the goods and set up a cake and cookie table.

"I will not throw up. I will not drop the cake. I will not accidentally smash the cookies or smoosh the cupcake frosting or lose any fondant lilies." This is the pep talk I need to be getting from someone else, like my nonexistent mom, but I have no one else here to give it to me so here I am talking to myself in Stella's SUV. "Lilah, you are not going to mess this up. This is the first step in the right direction for starting your business. You. Are. A. Warrior."

That might be taking it a little far, but I need to pump myself up. The fear of failure and going back to only dreaming about opportunities like this is too strong. I signal and slowly pull away from the curb in front of my apartment building.

Here we go.

The drive to the country club is short, but it gives me time to listen to some rally music and swallow my nerves. This is food, and food is my specialty. Pulling into the parking lot, it's just me and a few other vehicles. I'm not sure how many people are actually planning to attend, but I assume the van and other cars are for the caterer and staff. Brian and Stella and the kids were going to pick up Jenny and Dale since it's a surprise. Jenny thinks they're all just going out to an early dinner.

Parking as close to the entrance as I can, I leave the car running and climb out so I can start unloading. I put it all in here so I know I can easily take it all out. I prop the entrance open and yell "hello" into the dark room. Since the club is closed for a private party most of the lights are still off in the dining room and it appears there isn't a soul to be found when I stick my head in. The manager told me where to set up, and I grab a couple boxes of cookies from the back of the car and make my way through the building to a beautifully decorated table reserved for desserts. I make quick work of emptying the car so I can move it out of the way and, once parked away from the door, I walk in with the final cake box and set it on the table.

"You did good, Lilah," I say to myself as I carefully open the boxes and begin assembling the tiered cake. The decorations and color scheme match the frosting perfectly. I give myself a mental high five before popping in my ear buds and getting lost in the set-up, plating cookies and filling the cupcake stands.

I'm in my own little sugar-coated world and damn near drop a box of cupcakes when someone taps me on the shoulder. Yanking the bud from my right ear, I angrily whip around and stick my finger into the chest of none other than Guy with The Perfect Ass from the coffee shop. He's gorgeous and I immediately feel my face flame. Not because he's gorgeous, though. Oh, no. Because he almost destroyed a dozen cupcakes.

And I tell him so.

"What in the hell are you doing sneaking up on someone like that?" I screech. My heart is still in my throat. "You don't just walk up behind a person working on something like this and grab them! Do you have any idea how long it took me to make all of these?"

He takes a step back and I step forward, my finger still firmly planted against his pectoral muscle. A firm pectoral muscle. Very firm. I urge myself to ignore the feeling of it beneath my index finger.

Holding his hands up in surrender, his eyes widen slightly before narrowing again.

"What kind of person deafens herself while working on a dessert spread like that? I said hello multiple times and you ignored me," he says. Crossing his arms over his chest and pushing my finger away, he clenches his jaw. I notice the throb of his pulse racing along the side of his neck. "I didn't mean to scare you or almost ruin your pretty cupcakes, but I need that space. We're supposed to set up a carving station for the meat and that's where I want it."

"You're the caterer?" I question out loud. Like a moron. That's what I sound like. Of course, he's the caterer. Why else would he want to put a meat carving station right here where I've set up my cake table if he isn't the food guy?

"And you're the cake lady. What of it? You need to move the table."

This time, I cross my arms over my chest and stare at him. He takes a deep breath and rolls up the sleeves of his button-down shirt. I glance at his forearms and, well, let's just say my fleeting thoughts are not ladylike. But they're fleeting because he's a prick.

"No," I say, standing my ground. "This is where I was supposed to set up. The club manager told me exactly where, so you need to find a different space to carve your fucking meat."

"My fucking meat, eh? Fine. I'll set up somewhere else, but I'm taking this because I'm being so generous," he says, swiping a cupcake from the top of one of the displays.

"Put it back!" I yell. I know I'm about to make a scene and I kind of don't care. I worked so hard on this and it's my first paying job. The last thing I need is some asshole five-star chef wannabe screw it up for me. The worst possible thing to happen right now is for me to cry, and when I get angry that's usually one of the things to happen.

"Um, no," he says, stepping backward as he begins peeling off the fancy cupcake paper. I watch, horrified, as he pulls the cake apart and flips it together like a sandwich. Right before he puts the pastry between his lips, he smirks and says, "I bet this is going to taste heavenly."

My mouth gapes open. I'm having trouble believing what I'm witnessing as he takes bite after bite of a red velvet cupcake, leaving behind a smudge of buttercream at the corner of his perfect, stupidly delectable lips. Covering my face before he can come up with any smartass remarks, I turn away in an attempt to control my anger and keep my emotions in check.

"It's just a cupcake, Delilah. This isn't going to ruin your life. Stella isn't going to get mad that some jackass stole one of her mom's cupcakes," I say quietly to myself, closing my eyes to further keep the angry tears at bay. "I'll take it off the bill. One cupcake because of one asshole caterer."

The snickering catches my attention. "Are you talking to yourself? That's adorable. Stella's not going to care that I ate one of the cupcakes. She probably won't even notice if you don't say anything."

"That is not the point," I say without turning to face him. I don't want to look at him. I don't even remember what his name is from the coffeehouse but I already hate him. "It's no different than if I were to walk into the kitchen right now and make myself a plate of food without asking, the same food you've prepared for Mr. and Mrs. Barbieri and their guests."

"Sure, it is. It's wildly different," he says. I hear him wipe his hands with one of the paper napkins from the table. Finally, I turn to face him. I lift my left eyebrow and encourage him to elaborate. He sighs, placing his hands on his hips, and says, "Because I don't care if you make a plate of food before everyone gets here. I've been doing this long enough to not give a rat's ass about the leftovers, because there will be leftovers, and if you're hungry I'd rather you eat than starve yourself."

That is not the response I was prepared for. At the same time, though, in my gut I'm not surprised.

"Of course, someone like you wouldn't be worried about something like this. You probably aren't living paycheck to paycheck, praying you don't screw up and lose everything," I say, taking a step back and turning toward the rest of the food I still need to set out.

"You assume a lot of things about me, Pixie," he says. "Feel free to stop into the kitchen and grab some fettuccini and stuffed mushrooms to go with your meltdown."

Pixie? What the hell does that even mean? And did he really name call me? He doesn't know me. I'm still trying to come up with a comeback when I hear the swinging doors to the kitchen open and close.

He's right though. I am assuming things about him and his situation, but why shouldn't I? He assumes Stella won't be upset she's missing part of the order she placed with me. The first damn paying order I've ever had where I'm paid in money, not hugs and thank yous. There is so much riding on this one job, it's easy for me to believe a guy with an established catering business wouldn't understand or remember what it's like to be starting from Ground Zero.

I blow the tendril of red hair out of my face, put my music back in my ears, and continue my set up. Replacing the cupcake he took with another,

I will myself to stop acting like this one bad moment will turn into a bad day.

Chapter 6

Fisher

"Pixie? Where the hell did that come from?" I say to myself as the kitchen doors swing shut behind me. I don't know who this woman is, but she's got every nerve in my body buzzing and not even in a good way. Not entirely.

I cannot think about this right now, not when I have to finish getting the food prepped. Everything is ready for the most part, but we need to get the buffet table set up and start warming the hot foods so they're actually hot when it's time to eat. Cake Lady thinks she's the only one who has a lot riding on this event, but she's sorely mistaken. I've been in the restaurant business my entire life, but this is the first big event I'm doing as myself. The restaurant was Dad's dream and I love that Jacey and I have been able to keep living that in his memory. The catering gig, though, is all me and we're using Jenny and Dale's anniversary to officially unveil the name and logo.

"What do you want done next, Fish?" my head of waitstaff asks. She's been with us for as long as I can remember and has always been a loyal employee. When Jacelyn and I started planning for the catering side of things, we asked her to manage the staff specifically for the new business.

"Hey Doris. How are you holding up?"

"I'm fine, but you look like someone ran over your dog. If you're going to throw up from nerves, I suggest you not do it in here," she says. "You worry too much, kiddo."

Smiling at her, I nod in agreement. For years she had been a surrogate grandmother to us. When Mom and Dad died, she leaned into that role a little more.

"Why don't you grab a couple of the guys and have them start setting up the buffet table in the dining room," I suggest. "Stay out of the redhead's way. She's kind of a spitfire and I've already pissed her off."

Doris side-eyes me and smirks. "You? Piss off a nice young lady? Nah. I don't believe it for a second."

She settles in with her hip against the counter and, with an expectant look on her face, waits for me to elaborate. When she crosses her arms, I know I'm not getting out of this without telling her what a jerk I was.

Shoving my hands up into my hair, I breathe in as deeply as I can and release as slowly as possible.

"I went out there and told her she needed to move the dessert table after it was mostly set up. I wanted the spot for the meat carving station. Location is important." I pause and look at Doris. She raises an eyebrow. "And when she refused, I took a cupcake off her display."

Closing my eyes, I cringe. She must think I'm so juvenile.

"You took a cupcake? Fisher, that's not nice at all," Doris says, but I hear the smile in her voice as she tries to not laugh at how stupid I am.

Covering my face, I say, "And then I ate it like a damned Neanderthal. Right there in front of her, I took this beautiful little creation and devoured it. She was mortified."

"Why didn't you just pee on her leg?" Doris says, trying to breathe through her laughter.

I look up from my hands and my face must have said what my mouth wasn't.

"She must be real pretty for you to act so foolish," Doris says as she pushes away from the counter and calls out for help setting up the buffet table. "Don't worry. Ol' Doris will make sure you didn't ruin her entire day."

Leaving me alone in the kitchen, I can't help reliving the conversation. It's on repeat in my head as I check my watch and start getting food heated through. When Jacelyn breezes in through the back door, I'm shaken from my thoughts only to see it's getting close to show time.

"You made the cake girl cry?" she asks before I even get a chance to say hello. "Did you seriously take one of the cupcakes from her display? Working in this business, you know how important presentation can be. What the hell is wrong with you?"

"I didn't make her cry," I say, defiantly. "As for the rest of it ... Yes and I don't know."

Jace gets to work beside me heating water to cook the extra pasta — there's always at least one person in a group like this who isn't going to want the sauce on the fettuccini, so I try to make sure there's plain pasta at the ready.

"Emmy doesn't like flat noodles, so we're doing spaghetti for the extra," she says. "And you did make her cry."

"What kid doesn't like flat noodles? There's no difference in the taste," I respond. "And, no, I did not make her cry. You know, a watched pot never boils."

Jacelyn turns away from the stove and I see her eyes finally. She looks more and more like Mom as she ages.

"It's not the taste kids care about, it's the shape. And, yes. You did make her cry. Doris went out to start setting up and Delilah was trying to compose herself." Jacelyn pushes her index finger into my chest, much like Delilah did earlier, but it hurts when Jacey does it. I wince, but she just jabs harder. "Where is my super nice, takes food to the homeless shelter, plays basketball with the neighbor's kids, down to earth brother? You better find him, and quick, because that girl out there is hella talented and you will not destroy her fledgling career in this town."

I don't like this version of my sister. My head droops shamefully when all her words hit home.

"She's really pretty."

"That's your response? Don't be one of those assholes who turns into an asshole because you don't know how to talk to women. You talk to pretty women all the time at the restaurant, Fisher. That's no excuse for being a jerk."

"I know it's not. I was caught off-guard by everything when I went out there. People don't usually tell me no when I tell them to do something and she did. She had earbuds in and couldn't hear me at first, so I tapped her on the shoulder and it scared the hell out of her. My defenses went up when I should have been apologizing," I say mournfully. "Doris accused me of marking my territory and I swear that is not what I was doing. There wasn't anyone else in there, so why would I feel like I needed to claim her? I was not expecting this girl to have the effect on me that she did."

Hands on her hips, Jacelyn says, "You have to apologize. You obviously feel bad, so it's the right thing to do."

There is no time right now to go out and beg forgiveness. I check my watch again. People should be arriving. I'll admit my faults later.

"Did she have business cards? I'll grab one and call her tomorrow."

Rolling her eyes, Jacelyn places a rectangular piece of cardstock in my palm.

"Scaredy cat."

"Am not," I say as she walks out to the reception area. I'm not sure she even heard me.

*****

"Girls, where did you get these cupcakes from? They're almost too pretty to eat," I overhear Jenny say to her daughters as I stroll through the dining room. I've been checking on things throughout the afternoon, coming out from the kitchen to walk around and visit with Jenny and Dale's guests between bites and dancing.

I can't stop myself from jumping into the conversation. I'm not sure if it's because I think it'll make me feel better or because I honestly haven't tasted something so good in a long time. Neither of those reasons really register as I interrupt the discussion, though.

"They're not just gorgeous, they're delicious, too. It's the perfect amount of sweet to offset the cake. You could eat more than one without getting a stomach ache from the sugar."

"I heard you were the unofficial taste tester," Stella says, pursing her lips. "It's good they passed the Fisher test since I know how harsh a critic you can be."

"I'm not harsh. I'm honest. There's a difference," I say.

Stephanie squints and bites her lip. She's holding back. After spending as much time with this family as I have, I'm quite aware of how what I said can come back to bite me in the ass.

"It's not honesty if you're a dick about it. Then it's just plain mean," she says finally.

Stella smirks and Jenny gently swats Steph's arm.

"What? It's the truth, Mom."

I put my hand up to stop whatever scolding is about to go down.

"It's okay, Mrs. Barbieri. She's right," I smile at Steph, but I know it isn't a genuine smile because there's still that sinking feeling in the pit of my stomach.

"You hear that? Fisher said I'm right," she says, laughing. Turning to me with feigned concern, Steph places her hand on my forehead and then asks, "Are you feeling okay?"

I shrug and tell them I'm fine, then take off like I saw someone else I needed to talk to. The only person I need to talk to is myself. I mean, why wouldn't I be okay? I ate a cupcake created by a beautiful, talented woman and made her think I'm a Grade A jerk in the process. Totally normal … if you're a guy who has absolutely no clue how to talk to someone of the opposite sex.

For the rest of the party, I attempt to make myself scarce. I don't want to take the chance of running into the Cake Lady. There's really no reason for me to be out and about mingling with Jenny and Dale's guests when there are so many things I need to finish up in the kitchen. Since I'm technically borrowing the facilities from the country club, I and my crew are also responsible for cleaning up our messes. While the waitstaff is busy, I pull pans and start putting together takeout containers. There are plenty of leftovers that Stella and Stephanie have already paid for and, since they both have families, I'm sure they'd like to take home some of this food.

I work quickly and once all the leftovers are packaged up the pans go in the sink. We don't have a full staff for the catering side of things yet, so there's no kid to wash the dishes for me. This is busy work, though, and I'm not afraid to get my hands wet. It's nice to zone out a little and drown myself in deep thoughts and questions. For instance, why am I such a jerk? Why am I afraid to be in a relationship? And will I actually call that woman to apologize?

Apologizing means admitting I'm wrong, which I should absolutely do. But calling her also means having a conversation with her and I'm not sure I want to do that. Look how the first one turned out. What if I have to apologize for screwing up my apology? It would be easier to leave it alone and not attempt to make contact. Way easier.

M.L. Pennock

Chapter 7

Delilah

It seems like every other day there's another phone call from someone I don't know asking if they can place an order for cupcakes. I have Stella to thank for this. Without the anniversary party for her parents, not a single one of those new people would even know I exist.

"What are you daydreaming about now?" Maggie asks.

Catching me wandering off into my thoughts has become a new spectator sport for her. When I'm not in the middle of putting together an order from a grocery customer, I'm doodling in my sketchbook or staring off into space thinking about doodles I want to put down on paper as soon as I get home. This time, I'm not thinking about doodles despite my sketchpad being open and a pencil in my hand.

"I'm running out of space to work in my apartment," I admit. "I'm not sure if I can keep up with the volume of orders I'm taking without an extra set of hands or more counters. I might have to start telling people no."

I hate telling people no, but I love my apartment. It's just not big enough for me and a cupcakery. I even bought a shelving unit to store finished orders and all my extra ingredients.

"Have you considered opening a store?"

Shaking my head, I say, "I can't do that. There's not enough business to open a full store. Besides, I don't have the money saved up."

Maggie bites her lip and scrunches her nose as she thinks.

"If opening a store can't happen yet, what about renting out someone's kitchen? There's got to be a business you can make a deal with," she says. I see the wheels spinning but I don't know which direction they're going. Excitement sparks in her eyes. "Ooh! Ask Stella to ask Brian if he'll let you use the coffee shop."

Tapping the pencil against my bottom lip, I take it into consideration.

"I'll ask her. Most of the orders I've gotten since her parents' anniversary party have been from their guests, so maybe she and Brian would be able to help me out."

It's worth a shot, anyway. A long shot, considering Brian's specialties and mine overlap, but asking never hurts.

"In the meantime, do you have time to whip me up a dozen pink vanilla cupcakes with lavender buttercream for this weekend?" Maggie asks. I raise an eyebrow at her. I basically just told her I'm slammed with orders on top of also working full-time and she's looking for a favor. "My sister's birthday. She's not having a party or anything, but I wanted to surprise her with cupcakes and wine. I'd just order them from here, but she's kind of picky now that she knows you're advertising your talents."

Laughing, I jot down the order and tell her I'll have them ready for her on Friday. I internalize the rest of my feelings, though, because I don't want her to think I don't want to make her sister's cupcakes.

"You never did tell me about the party you catered. I assume it went well," Maggie says, the question hanging there in thin air waiting to be spun into a conversation.

I nod slightly as I reach for the flour. "It was nice. I met a lot of Stella's friends and family, and in turn passed out a lot of business cards, but I didn't stay the entire time. The family was certainly welcoming and asked me to join them for the party, but after my run in with the food guy I just didn't want to stick around too long."

Being busy for the last week has kept me from thinking about him. He never even introduced himself to me and I didn't bother asking his name. Hopefully we don't end up working other events together. I'm not sure I could handle that. Between his attitude and the way his pants fit, I'm not sure if I want to hate him or hate fuck him.

"What's wrong with the food guy?" Maggie's working next to me throwing ingredients into a stand mixer. I want to scold her for the way she's cracking eggs, but I'm her friend not her boss or her mother so let it go for the time being.

"There's nothing wrong with him, per se. He's just kind of an asshole," I say. I try to wave off the conversation by asking her to hand me the baking powder and salt.

"And?" she says, holding the salt hostage.

"And what? He acted like a jerk and I didn't stand for it and there were words and he called me a name, and now it's over and I hope I rarely ever run into him ever again."

She passes the salt, finally, and smirks.

"You think he's hot." A statement. I hate when she does that. "What name did he call you?"

Shooting her a sideways glance, I shrug and say, "Those are your words. I still think he's an asshole. He called me 'Pixie.' What the hell does that even mean?"

Maggie laughs loudly enough someone at the display case next to the bakery counter takes notice and stands there watching us for a moment before moving on.

"Yeah, well, sometimes the ones who are the biggest assholes also have the biggest hearts, so give the hot caterer a chance. And pixies are magical. It sounds less like he was calling you a name and more like giving you a nickname. It's kind of cute in a way."

"He ate my cupcake," I announce and she falls into a fit of giggles.

"I've never heard anyone complain about having their cupcake eaten, Lilah."

"Not that one, you pervert. He took one off my display and ate it. Right there in front of me like it was no big deal, he stripped her bare and devoured her. I was mortified."

"You need to get laid," Maggie says matter-of-factly. "Everything you say sounds dirty and fabulous."

This is why I have trouble being her friend and co-worker. "I don't think I need to get laid. But I do need to buy more batteries before I leave today," I say nonchalantly, knowing she'll think it's for my vibrator and not the TV remote.

"Dirty," Maggie says as she goes back to working on the pastries she's making.

I do not deny it, and shoot her half a grin before turning on my stand mixer and going back to baking. Popping my ear buds in I let the music flow through me as I frost a backlog of cupcakes, start on a birthday cake order, and check inventory to ensure we aren't running low on anything essential. Maggie flits around the kitchen, running back and forth between filling baking cups and assisting customers while I keep busy.

Quietly singing to myself, I don't notice him until my concentration breaks between songs when Maggie wanders into the back of the bakery. He's just standing there like he's waiting for me to see him, but I don't think he's noticed me at all as the doors swing shut behind Maggie. Yanking the music from my ears, I clear my throat loudly.

"What's up?" Maggie asks as she pulls a box labeled "Reilly" filled with fresh apple fritters from a shelf.

"When did that order come in?" I question, not wanting to ask her about the man who's picking it up.

"Couple days ago. He orders them every once in a while. Usually, it's for a Sunday pick up though, so neither of us are here when he gets them," she says, checking the order ticket. "Wednesdays aren't huge donut days here so I sort of side-eyed the order when I saw it."

She's so weird sometimes. Wednesdays are strange days to eat donuts? There are no bad excuses for donuts. Wednesday is just as good a reason as any other day of the week. Plus, apple fritters are the best damn donut out there. It's fruit in dough coated with sugar glaze and you just cannot go wrong. I'm more curious about the guy who ordered them, though.

In the span of a few weeks I've now seen this man a handful of times when I had never seen him around before. It's like he magically appeared to drive me crazy right when I'm trying to make huge changes in my life.

He's a test, isn't he? I ask the universe.

Of course, he's a test. Why else would I suddenly begin noticing him and have these horrific encounters with him. I'll just stay back here, working on this cake with yet another airbrushed cartoon character on it. There's no need to go out there and have a conversation with the Cupcake Thief.

"He's so pretty." Maggie sighs beside me as we both stare at the closed door.

"Yeah, well, he's also kind of an asshole," I mutter, turning back to the cake in front of me.

"What? No, he's not," she says, defensively. "He's been through some tough times, though."

I shake my head. "No, really, whoever he is, he's a huge jerk. I'm glad you're dealing with that order."

She narrows her eyes at me.

"I smell a story, but first let me get these out to Mr. Reilly. Then I want full disclosure," she says, turning and pushing her way backward through the door.

No, thank you. We are done with story time for today. The last person I want to think — or talk — about is the caterer with a gorgeous ass otherwise known as Mr. Reilly. I look up as the doors swing closed behind

Maggie and catch just a glimpse of him as he smiles at her and reaches for his order.

*****

With the bullet effectively dodged and no other mention of Mr. Reilly, I finish my shift and head for home.

It was raining this morning, so I drove the mile or so to work instead of walking. This is where I'm going to run into issues with big bakery orders. My car isn't huge, let's put it that way. Stella was kind enough to let me borrow her SUV for the anniversary party, but I can't rely on friends all the time.

Instead of going right to my apartment, I drive south out of town. I need to clear my head, especially after seeing him again. There's just too much happening and, while I know I could do more to control how I react, I feel like I'm being pulled into a cyclone of events and emotions and that's just not me. I've spent years teaching myself how to overcome things that stress me out. I am calm. I can handle life under pressure. There's not even anything I'm being pressured about ... except a new business I'm starting but don't know how to start, and there's the lack of space and excess of orders. Throw in the guy who seems to be showing up everywhere and my resolve is beginning to crack.

My car seems to have a mind of its own and before long I find myself at The Old Farmhouse. It used to be a working farm with a massive homestead but as the years wore on, the farm fell into disrepair. My understanding is there were no children to continue running the family farm and eventually, there was no one left to take care of the property. A few years back an out-of-towner like me showed up and purchased the property. Evelyn Winters has since turned a ramshackle, rundown, old house Into the premier country wedding venue and horse sanctuary.

I make my way down the half-mile driveway and fall in love with the scenery again. Flowing swaths of blue fabric drape between the large pillars of the white wraparound porch. White bows adorn the blue where the fabric is attached to the beams. Thirteen red wooden rocking chairs line the porch. It's as though they're calling for someone to come out and sit in them while enjoying a book and a tall glass of lemonade during the Fourth of July holiday this weekend.

The house was decorated initially for Memorial Day, but Evelyn is known for keeping the Americana feel alive all summer long only taking things down once Labor Day passes. Then it's pumpkins and Christmas lights until Valentine's Day. Since it's only the beginning of July, we can expect the red, white, and blue to remain for a couple more months.

The large horse barn in back is once again alive with animals. After getting the house gutted and remodeled, Evelyn remodeled and then opened the stables up for a local horse rescue to use. I park against the barn and turn my car off. Sitting quietly with the windows open, I listen to the absence of sound. I'm still not used to the absolute silence here. Growing up in New York City prepared me for a life of chaos outside my window. Here, I rarely hear chaos unless there's a rowdy group of drunk college students on the sidewalk beneath my apartment.

"Delilah, what a delightful surprise," Evelyn says from the corner of the barn. She steps out of the shadows, a set of reigns in her hand and a large chestnut mare following behind her.

Climbing out of my car, I close the door gently and pile my red tendrils on top of my head in a messy bun. "She's beautiful. Is she new to the farm?"

"Just arrived this morning. I wanted to give her the day to adjust to her new surroundings before walking the property. She's a little skittish and a lot malnourished, so needs lots of extra love," she says petting the short hairs along the horse's face. "What brings you all the way out here?"

"She sounds a lot like me," I mutter. "I just needed to get away for a little bit. The last few weeks have been overwhelming."

Evelyn smiles before nodding and walking toward me.

"Suddenly being the most popular pastry chef in three counties should make you feel that way," she says. Linking her arm through mine, we begin walking together down the trail that leads back to a hidden pond and gazebo. "It doesn't surprise me that everyone wants you to make their cakes and cupcakes. I've known for months how amazing you are, but kept my word that I wouldn't give out your name to my brides."

Dropping my head to hide my smile, I quietly thank her for not sharing my info with others.

"Can I please start telling them to call you now? Keeping you a secret isn't going to work much longer now that Brian and Stella had you do an event for them."

Biting my lip, I contemplate what that would do to my already overflowing kitchen.

"That's part of why I needed the drive outside of town. There are so many people who want me to bake for them and it's been a lot to process. Evelyn, I'm baking myself straight out of my kitchen. It's a small apartment to begin with and now, aside from my bathroom and bedroom, everything is for baking," I say. A nervous laugh escapes and I bite my lip again.

"I want you to know something. In the few years I've been here and have been open for weddings and big parties and whatnot, not one family or event coordinator for a business has had a local baker. They're all from the city. Small towns need small bakeries who do big things," she says. "The people who come to me for their gatherings should have someone who gives a shit make their desserts."

The skin between my eyebrows crinkle.

"I know of plenty of city bakers who care about their clients."

She waves off the comment.

"My point is, I like being able to keep things local. I've finally got the guy from Canalside Grill on my list of caterers to recommend, and I want to be able to put you on there for cakes and whatever else you create," she says.

"But what about my space issue? I've already blown my last paycheck on more shelving to free up counterspace," I say as we make our way around the pond.

Evelyn purses her lips and scrunches her nose.

"I have lots of space."

"I don't have the income right now to rent space though. That's one of the biggest snags I'm running into," I lament. "I downsized my apartment just to save money. I'm kind of regretting it."

"And if you did have the income? Where would you prefer to rent space?"

Main Street would be preferable, I tell her, but deep down I know those retail spaces are expensive.

"Well, for the time being, if you find yourself needing more space than you have in your tiny apartment, you call me. The kitchen is yours whenever you need it," she says. "Us transplants need to stick together, kiddo. Have you talked to your family recently?"

Shaking my head, I say, "No, I haven't had a chance to call. They've ended up with two new kids in the last couple weeks, so I wanted to give them a while to get settled before being introduced to the kid who aged out. I don't want them to think something like that will become their story, too. Is it weird I still refer to myself as 'the kid who aged out'? I've been an adult for a while now."

Aging out of the foster system without ever having a family petition to adopt me is hard. I'm relatively well adjusted despite that, but still I wonder why my last family — who I was with for six years — never asked to adopt me. I can't even remember there ever being a conversation about it, and I've held onto that from a long time. Maybe it's because I was already so independent. I haven't ever talked about it with Mom. "Mom" and "Dad," because regardless of being adopted or not, they're still the only family that stuck with me. They got me through. Even when I turned eighteen and could have been told to hit the high road, they let me keep my bed. They were the ones to come to my high school graduation. They helped me move into the dorm at college. My biological family and I haven't had any contact since I was nine. Not that I didn't try as I got older. They just skipped out on court dates and visitations. They failed me. It wasn't the other way around.

"I don't think that's odd at all. You might be nearing thirty, but you are still their kid. You might have aged out of the system but you did not age out of their family," she says, wrapping her arm around my shoulders. "Maybe call home this weekend. Then, come over and bake something fabulous to test out the space."

Chapter 8

Fisher

The door swings closed behind the bakery employee and I catch just a glimpse of a fiery redhead in the back. It can't be the same girl. I won't accept the possibility she works in the local grocery store. She's got way too much talent to be baking boring cupcakes people grab for their last-minute elementary school birthday parties.

Shaking the thoughts of the Cake Lady — Delilah, according to her business card and my sister, because of course she'd have a pretty name — I take my box of fritters and thank the woman for having my order ready.

"Not a problem. I was surprised you had an order for the middle of the week," she says. "I don't think I've ever been here when you've come to pick them up. It's always for a weekend."

Is she ... flirting with me? Maybe it's just a facial tic. I attempt to smile back at her.

"Usually I wait until the weekend, but with the holiday I wanted to get them early," I explain, though it's really none of her business.

I think she has something in her eye? She blinks way too much. I'm afraid my face is going to convey my thoughts and I try once again to walk away.

"That makes sense. Who wouldn't love donuts for the Fourth!" she says. "I'm more of a cupcake person. My co-worker makes amazing cupcakes and hand decorates all of them. They're so pretty sometimes I hate to eat them."

I stop in my tracks and turn back to the counter.

"Oh, really?" Maybe it was her hiding in the back after all.

"She's even started her own business. Would you like her card? Not that we don't want you to buy things from here, but —," she lowers her voice and leans across the counter, placing a business card nonchalantly on top of my donut box, "Lilah's a trained pastry chef and I really don't want to see her spend her life working in a grocery store bakery and making these gorgeous cakes as a side gig when it's really her passion, you know?"

The corner of my mouth lifts and I feel a little less grumpy about life.

"I absolutely understand what you mean. Thanks for the tip," I say, sliding the business card from the box and sticking it into the back pocket of my jeans where the one I grabbed weeks ago sits. I've carried it around while choking on my pride all this time instead of calling to apologize.

*****

Down at St. Peter's, Father Murphy welcomes anyone who needs a meal to stop by and eat with him every day. He doesn't make huge meals that could feed the masses, but he does make sure there's enough fresh bread and soup to go around. Today, he'll have donuts to offer as well.

"Fisher, what a surprise," he says as I walk through the church kitchen. "I wasn't expecting to see you for lunch."

I lift the box in a way to show I brought treats to share and nod in the direction of two gentlemen ladling soup into their bowls.

"With the holiday tomorrow, I wanted to come say hello and bring donuts for dessert."

Murph, as anyone who knows him calls him, walks over to the counter and pops open the top of the box. "Dale's apple fritters?"

"Dale's? Nah, these are from the grocery store."

Not long ago I learned about Stella and Stephanie's dad's secret rendezvouses with Brian at the coffeehouse where he's been making the occasional batch of apple fritters. He makes them for the Jumping Bean to sell but, like when my parents used to cook with me and Jace, I think it's a way for him to pass down that little bit of family legacy to the next generation. The recipe is one he's used for years that was taught to him by his mother and is just about the only thing he bakes. Dale's more of a smoke and grill guy, and I've bugged him relentlessly for his pulled pork recipe to no avail.

"I would say all apple fritters are the same, but we both know I would be fibbing," Murph says jovially. "We do appreciate the gift, Fisher. Will you join us for lunch?"

Looking at my watch, I nod, saying, "Sure. I've got time for a bowl. What have you made for today?"

Murph smiles, clapping me on the back, and nudges me in the direction of the stove.

"Tell us what you've been up to lately, Fisher. It's been a while since we've visited," he says.

"Well," I begin, setting my bowl on the counter. "I started the catering business, made a girl cry, and was told I need to start dating because my family is tired of me being alone or always the third wheel. That all sounds horrible now that I've said it out loud."

The chorus of chuckles gives me a reason to smile despite how ridiculous my life has been lately.

"You sure been busy," Will says. "I'm sure Jacelyn and Tommy don't mean they don't want you around, though. Your sister loves you too much."

Will, a local Army veteran, was instrumental in helping Jace get her art studio up and running. He looks like he's homeless — scruffy, rugged, clothes not always in the best condition — but the man is a saint. When Will first popped into our lives, he was just a face at the table we all shared at the restaurant on Christmas morning. It took a bit to realize how truly fortunate we are to have him in our lives. None of us knew he was Father Murphy's brother or that he's got a degree in structural engineering.

The concept that everyone in a small town knows everything about everyone else doesn't fit the Will mold. In fact, most of us who have gotten to know him over the years feel they broke the mold with him.

I eye him cautiously.

"She told you she was worried I would think that, didn't she?"

He shrugs and looks at Murph. I sigh.

"I'm too old for these games. What if I don't want to date? What if I'm content?"

"You just haven't met the right one yet. Tell us about the girl you made cry. That sounds more like the Fisher we know," Murph says.

Over the course of lunch, I share with them the story about the anniversary party and what a dick I was to Delilah. They laugh when I tell them about the cupcake and, in retrospect, I'm able to laugh about it, too. The guilt is still strong enough to cut my laughter short, though.

"I need to apologize to her for that. It was wrong and I should have acted like an adult. My nerves about making a good impression on the guests got to me," I say, picking at a thread on my pants. "Delilah seems like a spitfire. I think I'm afraid she'll not accept an apology."

Murph is listening intently. Will sits across from me with his elbows on the counter, fingers steepled beneath his chin as if he's also silently praying for me.

"Delilah? Like, the girl at the grocery store?" he asks. "That's the girl you made cry?"

"Her coworker referred to her as Lilah, though. I didn't know she worked there until her friend gave me her business card today," I say. The guilt creeps back in again. "But, yes, I made her cry. I mean, I didn't see her cry, but Doris said she was crying. How do you know her?"

Murph and Will look at one another and then turn their attention back to me.

"She's an orphan," Murph says. There isn't even a hint of humor in his voice.

I don't comprehend. How can a grown woman be an orphan? It's not like she's a little kid, or even a teenager.

"It's her story to tell. However, I will share with you she hasn't been here all that long. She's not a local and has no ties to the area. Tread carefully. She's definitely fiery, but she's had to be. She'll burn you if you aren't careful," Will says. "My suggestion is to apologize and see what happens."

Apologize and see what happens. I can handle that.

"Who knows, maybe you'll decide you like her for more than just her cupcakes," Will says as he lifts a glass of water to his lips, hiding a smirk behind the cup.

Chapter 9

JULY
Delilah

"I. Give. Up!"

This is such bullshit. I tried to make this lack of space problem work. I have tried to see the bright side of having too much business. I can't anymore. Maggie said to ask Brian about using his kitchen and walk-in coolers, but I didn't and now I'm ready to panic.

Staring at my overflowing shelves, I feel the hot tears of frustration as they begin rolling down my cheeks. I pull out my phone, find her name, and press the call button.

The ringing goes on for what feels like forever before she answers.

"Delilah, dear, how are you?" the cheery voice asks.

"Not okay. I'd like to take you up on your offer. There just isn't enough space here and I can't keep fooling myself. I'm overrun with orders. I've hardly slept since my last day off, and that wasn't even a real day off because I was filling orders," I say. "Please, help."

"No worrying, sweetheart. I've got space a-plenty for you. Do you need to come today to set up? I've got spare keys made for you already," Evelyn says.

I feel the smile spread across my tear-stained face, feeling the blessings rain down on me. I still don't understand how I ended up in this little town, but I am forever grateful for the people I've met since being here.

"You are a miracle, Evie. I'm going to get cleaned up here and then head your way. I have cupcakes to decorate and two cakes boxed that need to go into a cooler. There's only so much I can do with air conditioning and an apartment size fridge," I say. "Do I need to bring my stand mixer or is there one there I can use for the time being?"

"I've got one, but you're welcome to bring anything you think you might need," she says, laughing. "As I said, the space is yours."

Taking a deep breath, I say, "I just hope I'm not making a mistake."

"The only mistake would be to not go after this opportunity," she says. "Get your shit packed and get over here."

*****

Three hours later, I'm loading what I can into my Jeep and heading south out of town on Route 19. It's only been about a week since I was here last, but I feel like I haven't been able to breathe since leaving.

There's a large SUV parked near the main entrance as I pull up into the circle along the side of the house and climb out. My hair is piled high on my head to help keep me cool in the summer heat. My dress is super short for the same exact reason.

I open the hatch and pull a cakebox from the back of the car, careful to walk slowly so I don't catch my toes on unfamiliar ground. I hear his voice and it's too late to stop myself from turning in his direction. It's too late to steady the box in my arms and find my footing. There isn't even time to cuss as I trip over my feet and fall to the ground, landing on the stone driveway with the box just out of reach.

Laying on the ground, I can't even speak. Did this really just happen? Maybe it isn't as bad as it looks. The cake could be perfectly fine. I'm just going to stay right here and give myself a minute before checking the box.

"Do you need help?" he asks. "Are you hurt?"

Am I hurt? Physically, I'm in a little bit of pain from landing on rocks. Emotionally, I don't know how I'm going to recover from this. It won't be quick, that's for sure.

"I'm fine. I'm ... I'll be fine," I sputter, pushing up off the ground. Pulling my skirt down to cover my thighs, I brush the dirt and stones from my palms.

He touches my arm, lifting my hand to check for cuts.

"As far as falls go, that one was pretty graceful. I've seen worse," he says, quietly. I cannot even bring myself to look at him. How could this happen again? "Are you sure you're okay?"

"I will be. Excuse me, I need to check my cake," I say, and push away from him.

"Here. I'll help you," he says, turning to pick up the box.

"Please, don't," I say. "I've got it."

I lift the box from the ground and pray nothing has moved, not even one tiny fondant rose petal. It took hours to get this order done last night and now I find myself praying to St. Honore, the patron saint of bakers and pastry chefs, in hopes it will help put any misplaced frosting and fondant back where it belongs. Stepping toward the door, he reaches past me and swings it open. I rush through and set the box down, but it feels like I'm walking through mud with him standing there waiting to see how badly mangled the dessert might be.

I haven't even looked at him, afraid I'll completely lose my composure if I do. I really don't want to fight with this man again. Why is he here? And why is he hovering?

Holding my breath, I lift the lid on the cakebox.

"Oh, thank God. There's only a little damage," I say, mostly to myself, breathing out a sigh of relief. Taking the dessert from the container, I give it more attention, checking tips of flowers and all the corners to be sure the cake itself is still intact. I should be able to cover up any issues with a couple extra flowers. Muttering under my breath, I say, "You're so lucky this isn't destroyed."

"Why am I lucky? You're the one who tripped," he responds, standing up straighter as if I jabbed my fingers into his ribs.

Maybe I said it louder than I anticipated. Oops.

"I only tripped because you scared me," I say. "Why is it every time I see you, you're ruining something I've made? Why are you always ruining things?"

His kind demeanor fades and the asshole I met at the anniversary party is left standing before me once again. He draws his eyebrows together, the bridge of his nose wrinkling, and he lets out a disgusted laugh.

"I'm always ruining things? You're right. I'm a bad guy," he says sarcastically.

"I didn't say you were a bad guy, Mr. Reilly. I said you ruin things," I say, pulling my shoulders back. Feeling my anger flare, I add, "Since the moment I met you, you've been showing up and making a mess of all of this. Eating cupcakes that don't belong to you and now nearly destroying a cake I need for an event this weekend. If this was for today, I would be screwed and it would be your fault."

He places his hands on his hips, cocks his head to the side, and looks at me like he wants to say something just as horrible in response. He doesn't say anything, though. He just watches me.

"I've put everything into this. I can't even bake in my apartment anymore because it's too damn small and I need more ovens and more space," I rant. "Then you! You show up everywhere and fuck up my Zen. I cannot possibly concentrate and figure out what I need to do with you standing there staring at me like you're going to yell at me. Just … Stop pissing me off."

Lord, he's pretty. He makes me feel crazy. I say crazy things when he won't stop looking at me.

"Please, stop looking at me."

I'm so thankful there's an island counter between us right now. He looks like the kind of guy who would hug an angry bear, and that's what I am right now.

"I'm sorry." He says it quietly and for a split second I'm not sure I heard him correctly. He says, louder, "I'm sorry I have messed with your ability to do your job. I didn't know you were having a difficult time with your business."

That's not fair. He's not supposed to apologize. And I'm not having a difficult time with my business.

"Thanks for the apology, as backhanded as it is. I'm not having trouble with business, I have too much business for the space I have. That's why I'm here," I say. "Evelyn is letting me use the kitchen because I don't have room to do everything I need to do at home."

Why am I offering this information to him? I don't even know this guy.

"You're moving into this kitchen?" he asks, confusion marring his features. His absolutely beautiful features that match his voice and make things tingle in me that shouldn't be tingling. "That's not possible. I've got events booked out in this space for the next month. I can't have some crazy cake lady in here while I'm trying to prep for banquets and weddings."

Thanks, Universe, that quelled the tingle. This is exactly what I did not need added to my plate.

"Well, I am and it is and you will. Sorry about your luck," I say flippantly, hoping he gets the idea this conversation is over.

Looking down at the cake in front of me again, I assess the damage more closely. All my supplies are still in the car. I make a move toward the door, trying not to limp despite the pain in my knees from falling on gravel.

Mr. Reilly is still standing on the opposite side of the counter when I hobble back into the kitchen carrying a bin filled with baking supplies. He watches me with quiet interest as I pull containers from the bin and place them on the counter before turning and walking back out to the car.

Placing my hands on the back bumper of my Jeep, I take a deep breath and try to center myself. This is so not how I thought this opportunity would go. I pull my stand mixer out of the cargo space and close the hatch. I check the pocket in my dress to make sure my phone and ear buds are still in there as I walk back to the kitchen entrance.

"I see you met Delilah," I hear Evelyn say as I get closer. I stop before reaching the door and listen. Interrupting their conversation would be rude. That's how I justify eavesdropping. "She's a nice girl and you better play like a nice boy, Fisher."

"She's a pain in the ass and you gave her kitchen space without telling her she'd have to share it," he retorts. "I don't see how I'll be able to 'play nice' if she's going to take up my work area."

I hear Evelyn's heels click on the tile floor as she walks around the room.

"You know, Fish, it would serve you well to not act like an asshole. You're going to be catering events that happen on a single day, but you also have an entire restaurant kitchen to cook in and a big house to bake at. That woman out there? She's getting by running a bakery out of a one-bedroom apartment with a kitchen the size of a postage stamp," Evelyn says, defensively. "Not everyone is as fortunate as you have been. Especially after getting yourself into the debt you were in. Count your blessings and then share the bounty."

I think I've heard enough. This isn't me. I'm not nosy and now is not the time to become invested in other people's drama. Breathing deeply once more, hoping neither of them realize I was outside to hear them, I pop in my ear buds and make as much noise as possible while stepping toward the door.

Chapter 10

Fisher

She must be fucking insane. Evelyn gave this chick full reign over the kitchen like it's her personal playground. Shoving my hands into my hair out of frustration, I bite my tongue instead of lashing out at her when she mentions my debt. That was more than a few years ago and I've dug myself out of that hole.

"Count your blessings and then share the bounty," Evelyn says, as if I don't already do that as often as I can.

A noise outside catches my attention and I turn my head to look toward the entrance just as Delilah traipses back through the door carrying more baking utensils. I feel my features soften slightly when I realize she's limping. She's trying to hide the fact she's hurt and I actively put my scowl back in place because I don't want her knowing I'm not always an asshole. She's already made up her mind about me, so it wouldn't help anything anyway.

"Delilah! I'm so glad you're getting settled. Sorry I wasn't out here when you first arrived. Has Fisher helped you carry things in?" I shoot Evelyn a dirty look because she knows damn well I haven't. "He's a sweet guy, so I'm sure you two will have no problem working together when you're both here."

Delilah laughs nervously as she sets the stand mixer on the counter between her and Evelyn.

"I'm sure he is. We've met a couple times now, though, so I'm still forming an opinion," she says.

Fabulous. She's forming an opinion. Every time my sister takes time to form an opinion about a person it ends poorly. I don't know if I can work like this.

"Fisher has an event he's catering here this weekend. Will you both be able to maneuver in here or do we need to create a flow chart of some sort?"

Flow chart? No. And I'm not working in here with her during an event. Not happening.

"I just need her to not be in my way starting Friday night until Sunday morning." The curt tone to my voice is definitely not how I normally talk to people and Evelyn shoots a glare in my direction, a reminder to respect my elders.

"Not a problem," Delilah says. Folding her arms across her chest, I see the fight begin rising in her again. "I'll be fixing this and putting it aside until I deliver it on Friday afternoon. With any luck, I won't even have to come in contact with you. Fisher."

She says my name like it's a sentence all on its own. She punctuates it with curiosity and disdain rolled together. It's the first time she's said my first name instead of referring to me as "Mr. Reilly" like I'm some old man and it makes me crazy in a let's get naked and violate the sanctity of this space kind of way.

"Good," I say. I can't make other words work right now. My throat feels like it's coated in sand when I try to swallow. I watch her watch me swallow. If I don't leave this house immediately, I might say or do something I'll regret.

Without another word, I turn and make a beeline for the doors leading to the reception area.

"Fisher?" Evelyn calls after me. Before the door closes, I hear her say, "Well, well. That's certainly interesting."

*****

"Wait a minute … you just turned and walked out? You didn't say anything before leaving?"

Since I'm the man I am, I left and immediately called my sister once I was back at the restaurant for advice. She has none. We've been on the phone for a grand total of seven minutes and she's still trying to wrap her head around me leaving without even saying goodbye to Evelyn.

"You're rude. No wonder she hates you."

"I'm what? No, I'm not. I am not rude. She was angry at me before I even got an attitude. I was going to apologize for the cupcake incident even and —"

"You hadn't called her about that?" Jacey shrieks into the phone and I need to pull the receiver away from my ear. This is bad. "Fisher, I cannot believe you. Who are you? What have you done with my brother? I want him back. Of course she's going to be angry with you as soon as she sees you. Her last encounter was not a good one."

I hear Tommy in the background ask what happened and then the muffled sound of Jace covering the speaker on her phone so I can't hear their brief conversation.

"Okay, I've calmed down. A little," she says. "You need to apologize. A real apology. What the hell is wrong with you?"

Burying my face in my hand, I say, "I don't know. This is all so new to me. She makes me feel things, Jacelyn."

How is that even possible? I haven't known her long enough — or at all, really — to feel things. Considering I've never met another woman who has turned me into an alternate universe version of me, it's safe to say I'm feeling things.

"She makes me feel," I say again, quietly this time. "How do I fix this?"

I want my sister to tell me how to navigate this part of adulthood. It's uncharted territory for me. I have zero issues being a protective and loving brother, uncle, and friend. I don't think being Delilah's friend is in the cards for me if I don't make this right soon.

"You need to talk to her. Not on the phone. She'll hang up on you the second she hears your voice."

She said she'd be at the farmhouse on Friday. A plan starts formulating in my brain and I'm not sure it's a good plan. I won't know if it's going to backfire until I try, so I guess I'm going to also be at the farm on Friday, just earlier than I had originally planned.

"I have an idea," I say. "I'll let you know how it goes."

I have two days to figure out how to properly apologize to Delilah for being ... me. Murph and Will made it clear she had been through some difficult times in her life, and from the little bit she said to me about her baking thing it's still not easy going. I can work with that.

Chapter 11

Delilah

"Did he really just walk out without saying goodbye?"

Evelyn is as surprised by his actions as I am. I'm shocked more because I didn't think he could be a bigger jerk. Her surprise is more concern than anything.

"He did," she says, still staring at the door. "You fluster him. I've only known him a couple years, but I've never seen him behave that way. Fisher is a solid man."

"Solid? In what way? What I've seen of him he's kind of all over the place. Sometimes nice, but in a sarcastic way."

I don't mean to, but I let out a tiny sigh. It's so slight I don't realize I do it until I look at Evie and she eyes me suspiciously.

"What?" Why did I ask that? I don't think I want to know what she's thinking.

"Oh … nothing," she says. Clapping her hands together, she switches gears. "So, what else needs to come in? I'll help you carry things and get set up. You're going to love working in here. The windows really make this entire space come alive and the sunsets are gorgeous."

She's deflecting, and I'm okay with that. I've formed my opinion of Fisher and am not ready to change it.

We work through the afternoon to finish sorting the items I brought. Her kitchen is already fairly well stocked, but I don't want to outwear my welcome by using the pantry items she's purchased. She's already doing so much to help me simply by offering this space to work in.

"You didn't bring as much today as I thought you would," Evelyn breaks the silence.

"My car isn't really as big as I need in order to bring everything. Plus, I want to make sure I have a little of everything at home in case I have small orders I can do from there. My kitchen is overflowing at this point. I think I have every color food dye known to man and the pans are getting out of control," I say. I feel exasperated, but my face remains controlled and calm. It's a strategy I learned growing up. Don't let them know what you're really feeling. It's bad enough when I called earlier that I was so wound up and irate about my situation that I sounded half crazed. "What if this is too much?"

"Too much of what? Too much kitchen? You can never have too much kitchen. It's been my experience that most people don't have nearly enough kitchen for the amount of time spent in them."

I don't hide my smile. I don't stifle my laugh. She's right. Most people don't have kitchens that are large enough for all the theatrics that go into making all the amazing things one can concoct. Kitchens are magical.

"I mean, what if trying to get a business off the ground is too much for me to handle. I can't stop working full time because then I don't have the income to support starting this. Once this is supporting itself, then maybe I can cut back to part time. What if this all falls apart and people decide my cakes and cupcakes really aren't all they're cracked up to be?"

I can feel the fear of not being able to make ends meet begin to take hold. Money has always been my concern. It takes money to do everything — no home, no food, and no warmth if you can't pay the bills. It's been a long time since I was in a situation where I went hungry and cold. My biggest fear is ending up back there. It doesn't matter the last time I lived like that was when I was a child. Those memories stick with you, they create you, and they build your character.

"Wipe that scared look off your face, Delilah. No one is going to let you get in over your head. You haven't let your guard down much, but trust me when I tell you there are more people in this little community who will drop everything to help you if you need them than you could even imagine." She squats down to look in a cupboard and, just above a whisper, says, "I'm sure Fisher would be the first in line if he has his way."

"Ha! Doubtful. That man probably hates me. It's okay. I'm used to not everyone loving me," I say, but I smile.

"You just keep telling yourself that," she says. "Now, what's the first thing you're going to bake in your new kitchen? Have you come up with a business name yet?"

Evelyn and I meet at the island counter, each taking a side, and begin dreaming up plans for my bakery. She doesn't mention Fisher again, but my interest in the topic certainly doesn't go away. I still have an opinion, and I'm sticking to it until he proves I'm wrong.

*****

Thursday is a blur. Thankfully my brain is on autopilot while I work my usual morning and afternoon shift at the grocery store. I'm so worried about the cake I need to deliver tomorrow I can't seem to focus on anything else. It's for a birthday and while I wouldn't typically be concerned, this order is from someone I haven't baked for before. What if it's not what they were expecting?

Maggie comes dancing through the backroom where I'm filling another order for plain, old frosted cupcakes. Lime green this time for a school birthday party, with little football decorations stuck in the cakes.

"Those look like they're going to be a disaster if anyone is wearing a light-colored shirt," she says. "Sometimes I wonder why the parents don't just order white frosting and then customize with the sprinkles they want. We have plenty of football sprinkles."

"Who knows why anyone does anything, Mags? Do you need the cupcakes for your sister's birthday tomorrow night or Saturday?" I ask, without looking up from my task. "I have a delivery tomorrow afternoon, but I can bake tonight and decorate in the morning if you need them ASAP."

Out of the corner of my eye I see her shrug.

"Whenever you can."

No. That's not going to work for me. I stand up, piping bag clutched in my hand, and look at her sternly.

"Tomorrow is fine," she says, wide-eyed. "Are you okay, Delilah?"

I take a deep breath, the deepest I can manage. After getting her off the topic of Mr. Reilly last week, it wasn't brought up again. He bought his donuts, left, and we were busy the rest of the day. She doesn't know about the farmhouse.

I bite my lip.

"You're not okay." Maggie reaches out and touches my shoulder so I turn to face her. "What happened?"

Setting the piping bag down and closing the container on the finished order, I lean against the counter and unleash all the information I've been withholding. Which, it really isn't all that much once I'm done, but it feels like a lot. He takes up so much space in my brain lately.

"The conversations I have with him in my head where I'm explaining why I am the way I am and he's not mean about it ... I just wish he wasn't a jerk in real life," I say, sadly.

"He's really not, though, Lilah. He's a nice guy," Maggie says. "I think the two of you are misunderstanding one another and it's fucking over both of you. Why don't you call him?"

Shaking my head, I tell her I can't. That's more than I think I can handle on top of all the orders and trying to work out of the farmhouse instead of my apartment. I can adapt to most situations, but I don't want to adapt to the Fisher situation.

"You can and you are," she says. It's the first time I notice her cell phone in her hand. She hits the speaker button just as someone answers —

"Canalside Grill, this is Fisher. How may I help you?"

His voice makes my knees tremble. My palms feel clammy and I swallow because what else would I do when there's sandpaper coating it.

"I ..." and I can't get the next word out.

"Mr. Reilly? This is Maggie from the grocery store."

"Why, hello, Maggie. What can I do for you today? I didn't have an order for this week that I forgot to pick up, did I?" He laughs. He knows he doesn't have an order this week.

"Nope, but Lilah needs to talk to you. She's acting like a chicken so I guess we're pretending to be eighth graders and I had to trick my friend. Here she is," Maggie says, clicking off the speaker and handing me her phone.

"I hate you," I say angrily.

She rolls her eyes, but stands by for moral support as I place the phone to my ear.

"Fisher."

"Delilah."

I take another one of those deep breaths before continuing.

"I think we've gotten off on the wrong foot ..."

Chapter 12

Fisher

"I think we've gotten off on the wrong foot ..."

She's apologizing to me? This is so wrong on so many levels.

"You're not supposed to be the one to say sorry first," I blurt out.

Silence. I'm met with silence. I don't want silence.

"I've been meaning to call you to apologize for the way I behaved at the Barbieri party. It was not like me at all to react like that. I think I was just caught up in the need to have everything be perfect," I say. "It was the first event for the new catering side of the restaurant. I didn't want anything to mess it up."

She's quiet another minute.

Then, "Thank you."

Dead silence again. I try to not think about how the apologizing today is potentially going to mess up my apologizing tomorrow.

"What did you mean I wasn't supposed to say sorry first?"

"Well, when we met that first day you didn't do anything wrong. I acted like a major jerk, though, and —"

"Yeah, you did. I couldn't believe how arrogant you were. I still can't," she says, cutting me off. I can feel the big attitude she has through the phone and wonder just how shitty her life was before coming to Brockport to react like this to an apology.

"I know. That's why I'm admitting my mistake. Now, it's your turn."

I hear Maggie in the background begin to berate Delilah and instantly feel vindicated.

"Are you fucking serious right now, Lilah? Tell him you're sorry, too." She's not whispering, and I can hear her clearly enough it's like I was never taken off speakerphone.

"Fine. I will," Delilah says. "Fisher, I am sorry for reacting the way I did when you wanted me to move an entire display to make room for your meat station. I'm sorry for getting angry when you took one of the cupcakes without asking and shoving it in your face. My sincerest apologies for being mad about your voice doing things to me that made me trip with a damn cake. It's not your fault I lashed out at you when you tried to help me."

She takes a big breath. I would worry about her having more ammunition to throw at me if I weren't stuck on her saying my voice was "doing things" to her. Something tells me she doesn't even realize she said it and that makes me smile.

"So, yeah, Fisher, I'm sorry, too."

"Thank you, Delilah. It was nice to be on the receiving end of that apology. I don't even mind how you pointed out all the reasons for your reactions, particularly the part about my voice."

I try to refrain from laughing, but it's been a while since I felt pure joy where the opposite sex is concerned.

"I ... No. I did not say anything about your voice," she insists. "Did I? Shit."

"Yeah, Pixie, you did."

"Damn it!" She stifles a giggle, but gets serious again quickly and asks, "Why do you call me that? You don't even know me, so what's with the nickname?"

Scrubbing my free hand down my face, I feel the stubble from having not shaved in a couple days. How honest should I be here with her?

"You're feisty, Delilah, and magical," I say. "The cupcakes and the cake and the attitude and the red hair and the petite body ... you're magical. You remind me of stories about the fairies. Not the evil ones, though."

"Magical."

"Yeah. A magical pain in the ass that drives me crazy and not even in a bad way. Usually." I guess I'm going all in with the honesty.

"I need to get back to work, but this conversation has been enlightening," she says. "Have a good day, Fisher."

"Have a good day, Delilah."

The line goes dead. My lungs burn like I've been held underwater for too long and my blood pressure is sky high, but I feel lighter.

Maybe this isn't so bad after all.

"You got a stupid grin on your face," Doris says from the bar doorway.

"It was put there by a stupid girl."

Chapter 13

Delilah

Waking up early has always been easy for me. I have trouble sleeping in. These days I have trouble sleeping at all, really. Sometimes it's too quiet here. I grew up with the sounds of the city — honking car horns, fire truck sirens, the loud beeping of delivery trucks backing up. It wasn't until I was placed with my last family that I was introduced to a quiet suburban neighborhood on Long Island.

"How are things going with the new business? We miss you," Mom says as soon as I answer the phone. She doesn't sleep in either, and a phone call from her before 7 a.m. is not unusual. "Did I tell you we have a couple new kids? I think they would benefit from meeting you."

I'm not a coffee drinker, but I feel like even with getting up an hour before this call I could benefit from some caffeine. I break open an emergency chocolate bar before responding.

"I miss you, too." I put a piece of chocolate in my mouth. "Things are progressing. I have some orders to deliver today. That party I catered the cupcakes and cake for really boosted business."

Her response is not normal. It's a generic "that's good," and that concerns me. I lived in their house for enough years to know she's internalizing. We went to enough therapy sessions together for both of us to know when something is off with one another.

"Mom. What happened?"

Nothing much. That's her response.

"Mom, I know you better than that."

"They were in a situation a lot like you were before you entered the system, Lilah. But they're softer than you. You were tough before you came to us. These babies are just ..."

I put two more pieces of candy in my mouth.

"You need me to come home?" I'm offering more than asking, and it kicks me in the gut how much the word "home" affects me.

"Please."

"I'm on the first train out this afternoon," I say before being shoved into a memory that still knocks the wind out of me after all these years.

They all wanted babies and when I was sent to my first foster home, I was already wise beyond my ten years on this planet. It didn't take me long to know I wasn't anyone's favorite flavor cake. My first family kept me until I was eleven, when they realized my mother wouldn't be working to get me back. I went to the next house and was sent someplace else within weeks for reasons I still don't understand.

After a while, I stopped trying to get comfortable in new homes. Each new bed was just a bed, a plate at dinner was simply food. I had seen eleven different families by the time I was fifteen.

No one wants you forever after fifteen.

That last house was different. I felt it the moment I stepped through the front door. There was a vibe that welcomed me, wrapped me in her arms and gave me solace. I never got the impression I wasn't wanted.

"You must be Delilah," she said.

I pushed my red tendrils out of my face and refused to let her know I wanted this to be the last place I was sent. The Final House. That maybe I wanted it to be called home.

I reached my hand out to shake hers.

Her skin was soft, like warm leather, and I felt my hand tremble as she took it, wrapping her fingers snuggly around my palm.

"I am. I like to be called Lilah, though."

She smiled broadly at that.

"Then that is what you will be called. Do you like to bake, Lilah?"

The question caught me off guard, but for the first time in forever I felt a real smile form on my lips.

"Are you sure? I know you have a lot to juggle these days and it isn't that we can't handle it, I just think you bring a different perspective that they might be able to connect with," she says. "We're their first placement. They've been bounced around to temporary homes, but we're the first to offer permanent housing."

These are the first new kids they've gotten since I left home to pursue a future. It was out of left field, too, because I was pretty sure they had put themselves on hiatus with social services.

"Absolutely. I want to meet them anyway and after I take care of the orders I have today I'm free the rest of the weekend. I'll have to head back Sunday morning," I say, shoving the last piece of candy in my mouth. "Is there anything in particular they need or like to do?"

We spend the next several minutes talking about how the 11-year-old likes Minecraft and the 9-year-old likes reading fantasy books and drawing. I make a plan to head to the store on my way to the farmhouse to finish Maggie's cupcakes and pick up the cake to deliver in town.

"Perfect. I'll come bearing gifts."

"I know this is a lot to ask, Lilah, I just know you have first-hand experience. You've been through this and you've put yourself in a position to help other kids. You're the first person I thought to call. Maybe they'll open up a bit with you here," she says. "It's not like you're just a short train ride away at college anymore, either."

I hear what she says, but I also hear what she doesn't say. It's the silent, "We miss you," that makes me feel wanted. I don't always feel wanted.

"It's not like I live on the opposite side of the country, though. It's only like seven hours to Penn Station from Rochester," I say. "I'll connect to Long Island Rail Road from there and be Ubered home before midnight."

We spend a few minutes arguing gently in the way only my mom could about taking an Uber versus her picking me up, but I finally get her to concede when I remind her that leaving and then showing up at the house with me — a stranger — isn't really what these kids need.

"You're right. I know. I'll wait here, but text me when you get off the train so I can worry until you walk through the front door, okay?"

"You got it. I need to get ready and pack a bag before leaving for the farmhouse, so I'll talk to you in a few hours when I get on the train," I say. "It'll all work out. Believe me. I love you."

*****

It's barely ten in the morning when I pull up the long driveway to Evelyn's. A truck hauling a horse trailer is backed in near the barn and the same SUV from the day of the tripping incident is parked near the kitchen entrance.

"What the ..." I let the rest trail off.

I cannot turn around and go do something else until he's gone. For starters, that's rude. Second, I have way too many things to get done and not nearly enough hours in which to do them before leaving for the train station. Last, I want to see if his apology was real and not just because he couldn't see my face.

Pulling up next to Fisher's car, I park and just sit for a moment in the air conditioning before killing the engine. The kitchen door is ajar as I make my way up the short path with a box of unfrosted cupcakes for Maggie. Pushing the door open, I spy an empty kitchen.

Well, empty of people anyway.

There's a vase with a dozen pink roses sitting beside a teal stand mixer on the island. As I set the box of cupcakes on the counter, I'm surprised to see a card with my name on it slipped between the stems. Sliding it from its position, I carefully break the seal on the envelope.

"'Compassion is the fountain of forgiveness.' I read it on a tea tag, so I can't take credit, but it did make me think of you. Hope this mixer will be put to good use. Your work is incredible. — Fish"

I read it out loud a second time. When I say his name, I hear a sigh from the door.

"Now, that is the Fisher Reilly I've gotten to know," Evelyn says.

"Should I accept this? I mean, I have a mixer."

"And now you have a spare. He's a good man, Delilah. Accept the gift," she says.

Placing my hand on top, I try to decide which is more beautiful — the mixer, the flowers, or the man who provided them.

"You know he told me I was magical? It's weird, but not," I say. My face scrunches up as I try to wrap my head around yesterday's conversation with him. "Like a fairy. I'm magical like a fairy. As if I'm going to flit around sprinkling pixie dust on people. That's just silly."

Evie watches me curiously from the doorway, a small smile playing at her lips, as I begin pulling ingredients from the cupboard to make frosting.

"Maybe not pixie dust, but you've got the flitting about down to a science," he says.

I spin around to see Fisher standing in the door to the parking lot. My mouth hangs open and I feel the fabric of my dress swish around my legs from the sudden go and stop movement.

"I ... um. I was expecting to see you," I stammer. "I mean, your car is in the driveway, so of course you're here. Why are you here?"

"Event. Tonight, I have an event here. Remember? We agreed to not be in each other's way?" he says, his ears turning an alarming shade of red. "But I knew you would be here this morning and I wanted to surprise you with an actual apology instead of just the words. I was going to do all this anyway, but the phone call was sort of forced on us."

I roll my eyes.

"We have Maggie to thank for that."

"It's okay. I think it broke the ice," he says. Stepping further into the kitchen, Fisher holds his hand out to me. "Truce?"

Biting my lip, I question briefly if a handshake and kitchen gadgets are enough.

"Truce," I say, reaching for his hand.

I cannot describe what happens when he touches my skin. His hand is rough and gentle at the same time and I need to force myself to stop thinking about what they would feel like on other, more sensitive, parts of my body. My mouth opens to say something, and immediately closes again.

"Thank you for my gift, Fisher," I say finally. My hand is still clasped in his, his thumb slowly caressing the pad of skin between my thumb and forefinger in a way that makes my blood rush south of the border. My brain is sending up a mayday and begging me to get out of this situation despite how very good it all feels right now. I need to focus so I can leave town and this is the exact opposite of focusing. "You're not as much of a jerk as I originally thought. Maybe I won't hate you after all."

We pull away at the same time, and I feel the loss of his energy so deeply. I wonder if he feels it too as he looks down where our hands no longer meet between us.

"I'm just going to head on out and check on that new mare. You two enjoy yourselves," Evie says as she steps through the kitchen to the door.

I forgot she was there and I might be embarrassed if it weren't for the fact she was beaming when leaving the house. If she isn't going to make it seem awkward, neither am I.

"So ..." he begins, pulling my attention back to him. "Uh, what's on your agenda today? You have a cake to deliver. Is there anything I can help with?"

I tear my eyes away from his face, because staring is rude and I've already been unkind enough since our first encounter. Turning to the counter, I motion to the butter and confectioner's sugar.

"I need to finish cupcakes for Maggie and drop those off as well as the cake from the other day. You're welcome to help, but there isn't much to do," I say.

I detach the mixing bowl from the new mixer Fisher bought and take it to the sink to wash. He carries over the attachments and sets them in the other sink basin and begins washing them for me. The silence is comfortable.

"My parents started the restaurant. My first job was washing dishes in the kitchen. I think I was about thirteen," he says calmly.

"Did they pay you?" I ask, curiosity tugging at my ear.

He shrugs, rinsing the instruments in his hand, and says, "Not on the books, at least not until I was older. I was given a good allowance to help out when I was a kid and it taught me some decent money management skills, which is hilarious if you know my history with money."

Fisher laughs as if I'm in on the joke, but I don't know what he's talking about. My brain is stuck on getting an allowance and his parents being stable enough to own a restaurant. I wish I had that kind of stability at that age. For so many kids that's normal adolescence.

"I don't know what you're talking about, but if you were ever bad at finances it seems you've turned that around," I say.

Handing him a towel to dry his hands and taking one for myself to dry the mixing bowl, I step back to the island. I place the butter in the dish and the bowl in its seat on the machine, plug the mixer in, pop in the paddle attachment, and turn it on. I close my eyes as I listen to the whirring of the motor.

"I got into a lot of debt," he says above the noise, moving closer to me. "My sister doesn't know, but things got bad. Evelyn knows, that's why I mentioned my history with money. I just assumed she had said something to you."

I turn the machine off, the butter nicely whipped, and turn to stare at him.

"She never mentioned it at all. I think she respects you more than to share your stories with someone who hasn't earned your trust," I say. "Have I earned your trust already, Fisher?"

He's standing so close to me I can feel the rise and fall of his chest. Whatever cologne or body soap he uses is intoxicating, and I close my eyes to breathe him in deeply. It's a scent I cannot place, but it triggers a recollection of one of the families I was with for a short time and I smile despite them not keeping me.

"You're very beautiful when you smile, Delilah," he says softly near my ear.

I feel my cheeks heat.

"You smell like a memory," I say.

"I hope it's a good one."

This is when I'm supposed to tell him about all the families. He shared something intense about his life, and now it's my turn. But I can't bring myself to ruin it yet. Instead, I open my eyes and smile for him.

"It is. And now you're part of it too, even though I only hate you a little less now than I did yesterday," I say. "Can you please pass the sugar? If I don't get moving, I'll miss my train."

Handing me the confectioner's sugar, he also gives me a questioning look.

"There aren't any trains in Brockport."

"I need to go to Long Island today."

"That's a long way from home, isn't it?"

"It is home."

A lightbulb flickers to life in his eyes. "That explains the accent. You do a good job of covering it up."

I never thought I covered it up, I just pick accents up from wherever I am. Mom has never mentioned me losing the Long Island tone in my speech, so I hadn't thought about it.

"I once went to Virginia and came back with a slight southern drawl. Talking like you Western New Yorkers is nothing compared to that," I say.

He's stlll so close.

"Why are you going home? And why take the train when you have a car?"

"You ask a lot of questions."

"I like to learn about people." He dips his head toward my ear and I feel a chill travel down my spine as he says, "You're a people I would like to learn more about."

I swallow to try to wet my extremely dry throat as he pulls away and walks to the other side of the island.

"You're going to have to wait to learn more about me until another day. This frosting takes precedence," I say.

Flipping the mixer on again, I begin slowly adding the sugar and going about my business as he leans his elbows on the counter across from me. He watches my every move and when I'm done mixing, he hands me a piping bag and a box of new frosting tips.

"These aren't mine," I say, turning to the cupboard to grab the ones I brought the other day.

"Yes, they are. They're part of my apology," he says, sheepishly. "Look, I know how bad I messed up. Jacey said I owed you big time for being such an asshole and I agree with her. Please accept these tips as a token of my appreciation for not hating me for too much longer."

I slowly pull the case of tips from his hand and squint my eyes.

"Who said I wasn't going to hate you too much longer?"

Fisher nonchalantly rolls his eyes at me and shrugs, as if that explains why I would be less hateful toward him anytime soon.

"You're a distraction." I want him to leave but also not.

"I can go if you need me to. Actually, if I'm going to share the kitchen with you, I should start getting some things ready for tonight."

He smiles and taps his fingers on the counter, then turns away and walks toward the door. It's more a swagger than a walk, and watching him leave suddenly becomes my most favorite thing about today.

Chapter 14

Fisher

I hate leaving but, if I don't, I'm going to turn into an even bigger idiot. As it is right now, I'm pretty sure I'm acting completely opposite from how I was the last time I saw her. It's giving me emotional whiplash, so I assume she's feeling the same way. Maybe.

Once through the door, I find a quiet corner so I can pull out my phone and text my sister.

Me: How bad is it if I'm boiling today compared to freezing the other day? Even with the phone apology, I'm acting like a complete moron. There's no middle ground.

My phone immediately rings.

"What do you mean?"

"I mean … I feel like I'm acting like a giddy schoolboy. The other day I was being the jackass I was in high school," I say. Covering my eyes with my hand, I continue, "I'm so confused. This girl, I don't even know her and I want to tell her my life story. I went from yelling at her about carving stations and sharing a kitchen to fawning over the way she added sugar to a mixing bowl."

Jacelyn doesn't say a damn thing to make me less confused. She just laughs at me. Hysterically. Then I hear her gasping for air. And more laughing.

"Anytime you want to be done making fun of me, let me know," I say loud enough for her to hear over her own voice.

"You are too much, Fisher," she says. "You must really like this girl. Makes sense."

What the hell does that mean? I try to think back to my conversations with my sister about all the relationship things we've discussed over the last few weeks and I don't remember anything that would indicate why this makes sense.

"Remember when I said there was a girl who was watching us at the coffeehouse?"

"No. We haven't been to the Jumping Bean together in a lot of weeks."

She sighs forcefully — her irritated mom sigh — and mumbles something under her breath.

"What did you call me?"

"I said you're a stupid boy and no wonder you haven't found a girlfriend," she yells into the phone. "Holy shit, Fisher. I mentioned a girl from the coffee shop and that you should talk to the guys about the redhead who was there. You didn't bother, did you?"

Redhead? When did she mention that?

"You never said anything about a redhead, Jacelyn. I would have remembered that."

"I thought I did. Regardless, it was her. The girl was Delilah." Then she's silent. I wait. I don't know what to say. How do I say anything? "You should ask her out. Stop acting foolish and just ask her out to dinner."

I really should and it wouldn't be horrible to have a conversation with her in a non-work environment.

"I can't," I say. "I mean, I can, but I can't right now. She's going out of town and I'm not sure when she'll be back."

"You're an idiot. If you don't realize you can ask a woman to dinner more than a couple days in advance there is no hope for you. None," she says. "I need to go. There are things I need to get done that don't include me having to explain girls and how dating works to my older brother."

I hear her laughing as she hangs up on me.

Pulling the phone from my ear I say, "Okay, bye, I guess."

*****

Focusing on what I need to get done is difficult knowing she's working just across the room, but I try. We've been in the same space for thirty minutes and I haven't said anything else that's dumb. I'll take that as a win.

There's nothing holding me back from asking her out, except for me. I'm holding me back.

"So ..." I start without a map or directions or a location I need to end at. "Uh ... how long are you going to be down on Long Island?"

Well, it was a good run of not sounding completely stupid. Standing with my back to her, I silently chastise myself. If I turn around, I'll just get caught up watching her and get nothing done. I didn't actually have anything to do here this morning, but I needed the excuse to be near her for just a little longer.

Her voice is different when she responds and I do the thing I wasn't going to do. I turn around. She's bent over the cupcakes she carried in earlier, swirling the piping bag around the cakes, placing pale purple crowns on each one.

"Just the weekend," she says, her head still bowed in concentration, muffling her voice.

The room is filled with the scent of sugar and lavender. As if I can taste it, I lick my bottom lip just as she turns her head toward me. Her eyes widen and the curls stacked on top of her head bounce gently with the movement.

"I'm sorry, what?" I ask, clearing my throat.

Standing to her full height, all five feet or so of her, she repeats, "I said, 'just the weekend.' My family has a couple new kids and I offered to come help them get comfortable."

She returns to her task and I don't move an inch, because what?

"I'm sorry. What? They have a couple new kids? Like, your mom had twins recently new kids?" I'm confused and I'm not afraid to let it show.

Delilah laughs, the sound reminding me of the feeling I get when I hear windchimes in the spring, and for a moment I don't think she's going to offer more information.

"And done. Now, I can clean up and get these to Maggie. I would have been done a lot sooner if you weren't hovering," she says, taking her tools to the sink to clean up.

"Okay, justifiable, but can you explain the other stuff?"

"Foster kids, Fisher. I'm a foster kid, my family is a foster family, and now they have two new children who were just placed with them," she says above the noise of the faucet. Turning the water off and wrapping her hands in a dish towel, Delilah twists and leans her hip against the cupboards. "They're having a difficult time adjusting and I offered to go visit. I guess their situation was similar to mine."

Her situation which turned her into an orphan, from what Murph and Will told me. That's all they told me, though.

My mouth forms an O but I don't make a sound. I don't want to interrogate her about it and asking too many questions sometimes hurts. I don't want to make her hurt.

"What? I see a question. Just ask," she says quietly.

Stepping into her space, breathing her in, I forget how to use words. I feel such an overbearing need to be protective of her that I can't explain. Reaching out, I pull her to me and hug her tightly.

This girl … this woman I hardly know is going to ruin me. I feel pieces of myself tear away. All those parts that were pretend, the ones I put in place to protect myself after my parents died, begin to quiver because their foundation is unstable.

"No questions. You weren't going to share today and I'm not going to force you to," I say into her hair. "I just think it's really amazing of you to be so supportive of so many people."

That's when I feel it. Her arms wrap around my waist and I feel it. It's the pieces that were missing.

Chapter 15

Delilah

His touch is like fire. As much as I don't want to feel the burn, I need it and find myself burying my face in his shirt while gathering the fabric at his back together with my hands, gripping it tightly.

I don't just share information with people. I'm not ashamed of my past or my upbringing, but it's not something I advertise, either, because there are a lot of opinions about the foster care system that I just don't want to entertain. Telling Fisher was me taking a chance I wasn't ready to take, but it seemed like a necessary step in whatever this is we're doing. Our friendship. That's what we're doing. We're having a friendship.

But I still hate him a little.

I hate that he's making me feel certain things I don't want to feel. I'm supposed to be focusing on this new business. That's what I should be doing. Instead, I'm focusing this second on the way he makes all the best parts of me tingle.

He breathes in deeply. It's the first time I realize how much taller he is than me. Slowly I lift my head away from his chest.

"Are you sure you don't have any questions?" I say quietly. "Usually when people find out I was in the system they have a thousand thoughts and want to tell me how they once knew a kid who knew a kid who was placed with a family. Then it spirals out of control into nothing but bad shit about foster care."

He tips his forehead down to touch mine, closing his eyes, and says, "Nope. You're obviously private about it for a reason and I don't want to force you to tell me anything you don't want to share. Plus, I have zero preconceived notions about foster care. Everyone has a history. Everyone has a past."

I didn't think a person making an admission like that could make me feel breathless. When I close my eyes, I feel him pull away but not very far.

"Would it be weird if I kissed you?" he asks.

"I don't know. It's been a long time since I was kissed," I say, swallowing the lump in my throat.

He cautiously presses his lips against my forehead.

"I like you Delilah," he whispers against my skin. "When you get back from visiting your family, I would like to take you to dinner if you're up for it."

Am I up for it? Dinner with someone who isn't Maggie or Evelyn? I know I'm taking a lot of time to respond, but dating hasn't ever been a big thing for me, mostly because boys in high school and college didn't seem to know what to do with me and men usually think I'm too much for them.

"You don't have to answer me now. I can wait," he says.

"Are you sure? You don't seem like the kind of man who likes to wait."

We pull back at the same time, and he smiles broadly at me.

"I can wait for you."

*****

Fisher loaded the couple of boxes into my car that needed delivering and sent me on my way, but we hardly spoke again before I left, with the exception of him giving me his phone number.

I felt weird not hugging him before departing and I'm a thousand percent sure that's not how I'm supposed to react to a guy I swore to hate forever a week ago. Now I have had hours to think about it while on the train. As I pull into the station and grab my backpack, I miss him. I haven't missed someone in years. Not like this. There's also never been a person I'm attracted to the way I'm attracted to Fisher. It isn't just a physical attraction; it's mental.

Stepping onto the platform, I pull up the app on my phone to find a ride as I make my way toward the entrance. The station is practically empty at this hour and a small part of me wishes I had just let Mom pick me up. I'm not afraid — much — but it can be a bit unnerving to be alone in the dark at the train station. Thankfully, the car scheduled to drive me home arrives within minutes and I climb in beside the driver knowing I'll be at the house momentarily.

"Thanks so much," I say, stepping out of the car with my bag clutched to my chest.

He wishes me a good night and drives away, leaving me standing on the sidewalk staring at the house that was just a house until the people inside turned it into a home.

"They're just children. Nothing to worry about. I'm only here to help them adjust. There's no harm in trying," I say. "Nothing says any of us are going to get attached."

I've done this a thousand times before. Walking up the path to the front door isn't anything new for me. But this time it feels a bit like I've been replaced. Granted, I grew up and moved on, so replaced may be an extremely rough word to describe the feeling. Reaching for the doorknob, I don't have time to and can't think of another one to use.

"You're here!" she exclaims before the door clicks into place behind me.

She pulls me into a hug that speaks a million emotions in one gesture and it's almost more than I can handle. There's been a lot of stress lately and I haven't had a good outlet. She was my outlet for all those big years.

"I'm here," I say, trying to breathe through the vise grip around my shoulders and the grin I can't contain.

Mom loops her arm through mine and pulls me further into the house, her smile infectious.

"Come. The kitchen is calling and there's a fresh pan of macaroni and cheese waiting for you."

We walk into the same kitchen that welcomed me all those years before, only it's been updated since that first night. As we learned to cook together, we decided getting rid of outdated appliances would be a benefit to all of us and any other children they homed. As a teenager, I truly felt like they did it just for me. Sometimes it felt like an apology for where my own mother fell short, other times it felt like I was the one pushing them to be better.

"Are they sleeping?"

Placing my bag on a kitchen chair and opening the top zipper, I slip two small packages out. Gifts. I always wished when I went to a new family, they would have given me something to help make the transition feel like I was more than just another mouth to feed. Aside from Dan and Julie, there was only one other family who welcomed me with a survival kit of sorts. Knowing Mom had kits ready for the new kids gave me the chance to buy something fun.

Mom sets a bowl of homemade mac and cheese in my hand and kisses my temple.

"Passed out cold. They had a big day. Meeting with the social worker to make sure they were settling in, big talks about starting therapy to get the feelings out. You know the drill," she says with a meek smile. "It's been hard on them, but I told them both you were coming to visit and it seemed to put them at ease."

I nod my head as I chew a mouthful of food.

"I didn't know if you were going to tell them I was coming," I say, wiping cheese from my lips with the napkin she hands me.

"I mentioned our daughter and Genevieve saw your portraits on the wall, so the questions started," she says, shrugging as if that explains everything. "Once she knew how you had come to be our daughter, she started feeling a little more validated. I think that's the word I want. She just needed to know she wasn't alone. As far as Jaxon is concerned, you're just another adult he's going to have to meet. If he's a bit shy at first, it's probably not you."

I cling tightly to her use of the word "daughter." I've never been formally adopted by them, but they kept me.

"Have you figured out the apartment issue?" she asks.

I look up from my bowl.

"Uh, not yet. They haven't tried placing anyone with me, but the social worker I'm matched with is aware of the situation," I say. "Now that the bakery business is taking off a little, I should be able to get back into a two bedroom by the time my lease is up."

Mom picks up a mug of tea and takes a cautious sip. I can tell she's been thinking.

"I'm afraid you're not going to leave here with your whole heart, Lilah."

Her words are a warning I wasn't expecting, but I take heed as if my life depends on it.

*****

It doesn't feel like I was gone for an entire weekend, but before long I'm repacking my bag and wrapping my brain around how traumatic my childhood was for me. That's what this trip home was — unpacking trauma. Not that I haven't had years to do that in therapy and through journaling, but it's different when you're looking at kids who were you and know you've been through a lot of the same things. The biggest difference is they haven't been bounced around from one family to another. I'm thankful this is their first placement. I'm thankful they have Julie and Dan ... and me.

"Will you be back?" she asks from the door, watching my every move.

This is the part I'm scared of. I came into their lives for just a couple days and now I'll leave, and my concern is them feeling that abandonment all over again. Their mother did it first. She left them to fend for themselves until the neighbors caught on, got concerned, and inserted themselves into the situation.

"I could come back and visit. Are you going to be here if I do?"

"I wanna be. I like it here. So does my brother."

"Well, Genevieve, I suppose I could make plans to come back sometime soon," I say. Sitting down on the bed in my room, which is now her room, I feel her guard slip back into place a little. "You can always call me. Mom has my number and I'll let her know the same."

I didn't expect her to hug me so tightly. I don't know what I did expect, but it wasn't that. By the time I was placed here, I had been let down by so many people there was no letting myself get attached too quickly. I didn't hug anyone for a long time.

"Why didn't your mom come back for you?" she asks as she sits down beside me.

The question is so quiet but she might as well have screamed it in my ear. I take a minute to think, because I don't know the answer and it isn't a question I thought an 11-year-old would ask. Her 9-year-old brother? Absolutely. I feel like before a kid turns 10, their filter isn't in place yet. Regardless, I'm not prepared for this.

"I wonder that sometimes. Sometimes I think I should go visit her. Then I stop wondering and thinking and start feeling thankful, because what would it have been like if she had? Would she have been ready to be a mom? Would she have gotten clean to get me back just to fall back into that trap again?" Picking at the skin around the nail on my index finger, I collect my thoughts quickly. "Genevieve, I don't know why she didn't come get me, but I'm happy every day that I was finally given this family, because this family taught me love and accepted me with all my hard lines and scars and rough edges."

"I don't want my mom to come back," she says point blank. I don't think she intended to say it and the shock of the admission shows in her eyes. "We didn't feel … safe. Or liked. There was no love. There was no love and then she just stopped coming home, so it was just me and Jax. Before the old lady next door called the cops about us, I was all he had for a long time."

Pulling her closer to me, I say, "You did a good job, Gen. You kept him safe. You showed him how to love. Without you, Jax wouldn't know those feelings. Do me a favor, okay?"

She nods but doesn't look at me.

"Take Mom up on the idea of talking to someone. A counselor at school or a therapist who can see you on a regular basis. I balked at the idea when I was your age. I hated thinking about telling someone all my secrets and my fears. But … once I did, I also was given a safe place to tell someone my dreams and my plans for my future."

"Is that how you got to go to college?"

Tipping my head down and laying it gently on top of hers, I smile. I like this memory.

"I got to go to college because I worked really hard and Mom and Dad believed in me," I say. "But more than that, I believed in myself."

Chapter 16

Fisher

So, there I was, standing in the driveway watching her drive away with a car load of cupcakes and a cake and parts of my heart I didn't want to admit were slowly beginning to belong to her. I sound like a giant man-baby, but in this short amount of time her mouthy mouth and fiery spirit has done something to me that no one else has.

She's made me feel alive.

I don't know how I survived my event on Saturday after spending the previous morning sharing space with her. Doris called me out repeatedly for losing focus, I couldn't stay on task, and the only saving grace was I didn't spend much time outside of the kitchen.

Now that I haven't seen her in almost three days, I'm trying to figure out how creepy it would be to call her and see if she's back yet. Delilah said she was only going to be gone for the weekend, but did that mean she was coming back Sunday or staying Sunday and coming back Monday? I should have asked.

I look at my phone again and say, "Fuck it." Opening the messaging app, I start a new text.

Me: If you're free Wednesday night, I'd like to take you to dinner.

Then I immediately delete it and set the device down. It's only five-thirty in the morning. Texting anyone this early is just cruel. I do something any sane person would do who is obsessing about another person — I Google her. Then I scour her social media. What I find is a girl who loves all music, baking, hot chocolate, and puppies. She shares posts about mental health and inclusivity. She's passionate about everything.

And I wonder how much of the real her she shares with other people.

This time I don't delete the message. I type it and send it, put my phone down, and go take a shower where I think about her some more, in a less G-rated way.

Chapter 17

Delilah

Fisher the Jerk: I want to make you dinner. Wednesday if you're free. My house or yours, you choose.

I would normally be upset with a wake-up text at six in the morning when I didn't get in until after one, but I wasn't really sleeping anyway. He's been on my mind since I got on the train back to Rochester, then the drive back to Brockport was consumed by him. I was able to clear my head for the weekend. Not being in the same part of the state as him made that easy.

Dinner made by him, though? It's not like I haven't been alone with him, but this would be different ... somehow.

I pick out a new dress I found at the thrift store and braid my hair. At almost seven I finish getting ready and grab my phone on the way out the door without responding to him.

*****

"You didn't text me back."

I'm leaving the store after work and answer my phone without looking at the caller ID first. Hearing his voice makes me stop in my tracks.

"I — I was going to. I just got busy and didn't have a chance," I lie and immediately regret it as the knot forms in my stomach.

The truth is, I thought about him all day long. Sometimes it was how much he irritates me. A lot of times it was nothing more than fantasies of what dinner would include and if there would be dessert after if I said yes to Wednesday. Except dessert would be each other. And of course, I'm going to say yes. How much more does the universe need to do to make me just accept the fact this needs to happen? Not necessarily sex, but spending time with him. If I wait until I have the courage to try something new, I'll never attempt a thing.

"I'm sure you were. What time did your train get in?"

I smile and begin walking again, letting the late July sun shine down on my face.

"Around midnight, but I didn't get home until after one. It was a short night," I say.

"And then some asshole started texting you at the crack of dawn, right?"

"It's like you're reading my mind. But, I've been told he's not really much of an asshole and I wasn't sleeping when I got the message anyway, so it isn't like his timing was horrible," I say.

He's quiet for a moment and I almost let myself start to worry. It's a major shift from not caring what he's thinking to hoping he's not thinking he shouldn't pursue whatever this is between us.

"I'm glad the timing wasn't horrible," he says, his voice deeper than it was a moment ago. "Are you free Wednesday? I don't know if there's a chance we'd see each other before then because of schedules, but if you can swing mid-week, I'd really like to spend some time with you."

"You want to cook for me?"

"I do."

Man, that's a nice phrase. The thought is fleeting, but it makes my heart skip. This is just dinner, Lilah, not a fucking marriage proposal. I try to regain my composure as I continue walking down the sidewalk toward my apartment.

"Then I think me coming for you would be best," I say.

"Coming for me, eh? I like the sound of that."

"What? No. Oh God. Coming to you. I'll come to your house. Shit," I ramble, hardly believing I slipped while talking to him. Again. This isn't the first time.

"It's my voice isn't it?" he asks, but I can tell he's trying not to laugh.

"Goodbye, Fisher," I say a little too loudly so he can hear me over his laughter. "Text me your address and I will see you Wednesday."

I end the call as I walk past the Jumping Bean. Without a second thought, I slip inside and order myself a salted caramel mocha latte because what's a little extra sugar to go with my heart palpitations?

"You don't usually get coffee drinks when you come in, Lilah," Greg says from behind the counter. "I think you're going to love this one though."

I hand him my money and place the change in the tip jar as he turns to start prepping my drink.

"I figured today was a good day to try something new."

Chapter 18

Fisher

"I don't know what I'm doing. I have never before cooked for a woman. Ever."

"Lies. You cook for women all the time," my sister retorts. Sometimes I hate her a little bit.

"Cooking for a group of grandmas on a Friday night is different than cooking for a goddess my age."

I hear her sigh deeply, and it sounds ominous when on speakerphone. It's one of those deep ones where I'm afraid she's going to forget to breathe. I'm being absurd and I know I am, but I thought she and Tommy were crazy thinking I needed to start dating. Now, here I am trying to get food prepped in the kitchen I watched my parents cook in together. Maybe I should have had her come over earlier to help?

"Goddess? Fisher, she's a normal human being just like you. She likes to eat normal food, not the souls of her enemies. What are you making?"

I tell her I have a roast resting in the warming pan, already sliced so it's ready when Delilah gets here, and she's very quiet.

"What's wrong? Why not roast?"

"There's nothing wrong with roast. Roast is good. It's a good 'come home and meet my family' kind of meal," she says, but the words don't match her voice and I can't pinpoint what's wrong until she says, "Make sure you pair it with the right wine."

I stop mixing the custard for the crème brulee and smile.

"Red or white?"

"Either. They both get the job done."

"I miss them too, Jace. I didn't even think about the roast having any sort of meaning when I picked it."

The last meal we shared with our parents before they died was a huge roast beef dinner with all the trimmings, but our mom's favorite thing was to remind Dad to pair the wine properly. She never cared which one went with the beef and would tell him, "They both get the job done."

"It's okay. I think it's a good way to make sure she's good for you."

I hear a faint knock at the front door and my head shoots up.

"She's here," I whisper. "I have to go."

"Have fun. Don't do anything to make it awkward. I love you," she says, and then the line goes quiet.

I wipe my hands on the kitchen towel hanging from the waistband of my jeans and move quickly through the house to get to the front door. Right before opening it, I say a silent prayer that I don't fuck this up and will my heart to stop racing.

"I can see you. Are you going to open the door?" she says from the porch.

The words are followed by the sweet melody of her laughter. I let out a laugh of my own as I open the door and come face to face with the only person to come close to being the woman of my dreams. We stare at one another for a beat before I remember my manners and ask her to come in.

"Thought you'd never ask," she says.

I lead Delilah through the house, reaching the kitchen as I tell her how we rarely use the front door. I apologize for forgetting to tell her to come to the back door, but she doesn't even seem phased by it. Her eyes are wandering around the room.

"This kitchen is gorgeous," she says.

"Thank you. It was my parents' favorite room. We spent a lot of time in here," I say.

The rush of memory lane hits me hard between talking to Jacey about roast and wine, and Delilah's obvious appreciation for the room that always brought us together.

"We're kitchen people."

She smiles and it reaches her eyes, the green of them seeming more vibrant with my admission.

"Me too. That's what made me feel comfortable when I went to live with my last foster family," she says. Shrugging her shoulders, "It was the first room I spent any time with my foster mom in, and as much as I already loved baking, she really gave me the chance to explore and create."

I round the island counter and finish preparing the crème brulee for the oven. I want her to keep talking. There's something there and it feels like she needs someone to talk to as much as I do.

"This is the family you went to see last weekend?" I ask, hoping it opens the door.

She leans her elbows on the counter, making herself at home, and watches me with rapt interest as I place the custard dishes on a cookie sheet before opening the oven and setting them on the rack inside.

"You're doing it wrong."

"Excuse me?"

"You're doing it wrong. They should be in a water bath so the custard doesn't crack. That's what makes them so creamy. The water helps the heat move through the dish more evenly," she says.

I stare at her a second longer, and then pull the pan back out of the oven.

"All you need is a nine-by-thirteen baking pan. You do have one of those, right?"

"I have several. You might say, I have a collection."

Smiling, but trying not to laugh at me, Delilah says, "I'm sure you do."

She gathers her hair, pinning it up in some fancy twirl with bobby pins she pulls from her pocket, and moves gracefully around the counter to stand beside me.

"I've never actually made this before. Not this part. Doris makes them for the restaurant. I just put the sugar on and torch them when they're ordered."

I feel like a fraud — what food guy who owns a restaurant has never made this dessert? This guy. Shameful.

"Can I help? This is kind of my specialty."

"Absolutely," I say.

The blood rushes in my ears, the whoosh of emotion hitting me so forcefully and I'm almost absolutely certain it's not just a physical attraction anymore. The only other women to cook in here were my mom and my sister. It's surreal how she's settled my nerves after spending all day being nervous for this evening. I never thought I would be affected the way I am right now watching her move so effortlessly through the room as I hand her a baking dish. She takes care of the rest of the prep, maneuvering around as if she's been here before. The entire time, she's filling me in on who she is and talking about her family.

"To answer your question from before, yes that's the family. They were the last ones to take me in after, um, a lot of other placements," she says quietly while closing the oven door. The lack of number in her statement isn't lost on me. "I wasn't a bad kid. No one wanted to take in a kid who could take care of herself. Everyone wanted babies. Babies were adoptable. An almost teenager? Not so much."

"Eh, babies are only cute for so long. The real fun starts when they're older, anyway."

Rolling her eyes and smiling at me again, but this time it's a smile that touches all the way to the very middle of my chest, she says, "And what do you know about babies?"

"Lots. My nephew is basically the center of my world. Jace and Tommy sometimes think I'm a third wheel, but really I like being there to spend time with Jonah," I say, pressing my finger into a small pile of sugar. "He was boring when he was tiny, though. Now that he's getting into things, I'm looking forward to when he's older and I can do cool uncle things with him."

"But what about when he's fifteen? And hormonal and moody?"

Delilah watches me carefully, waiting for my reaction to her questions, but I keep my face neutral.

"Well, I hope I'll be like my dad was with me, only not the dad. Level-headed, calm, and a great listener who can offer the advice he needs that maybe he isn't ready to talk to his dad about."

The thought is fleeting, but a small part of me wonders if she knows her father.

"You'll make a good father someday. Until then, you seem to be an awesome uncle," she says.

Her eyes are wistful, and I wonder what memories she's trying to escape. When Jacey looks like that, she's usually thinking about all the experiences we missed out on with our parents. We had a childhood with them, though. Delilah doesn't seem to have had that, at least not with her own family.

"What are you thinking about?"

She shrugs, but I know there's more.

"Want me to be mean to you again? You have no problem talking to me when I'm being a jerk, so if you need a little inspiration, I can give it to you."

"My family. Not my foster family. The other one. I'm sure you have questions," she says. Walking over to a cupboard she points and asks, "Glasses?"

I shake my head and move around the counter to pull a cup from the correct cupboard. Handing it to her, her fingers brush mine and I can't help the want to kiss her. But I don't. I respect her enough to go at her pace.

"Thank you," she says quietly.

"You're right, you know. I have questions. The thing is, I know to not ask them until you're ready to answer them."

"I think I'm ready to answer them."

Here goes nothing, right?

"Would you like red or white with the roast?"

She scrunches her eyes and it wrinkles her nose. So, being the mature adult I am, I boop it.

"You thought I was going to ask something else, didn't you?"

"I did. I wasn't expecting that. However, I like both even though I don't drink often. I'm more of a 'they both get the job done' kind of girl. Just don't expect me to have more than one glass. I have to drive."

I'm not entirely sure I heard her correctly, so I ask again. Eventually she's going to think I'm hard of hearing.

"They both get the job done."

Walking to the wine rack, the stupidest grin on my face, I pull a merlot from my stash.

"Red it will be, then."

The roast has been ready, the table is set, and I'm starving for more conversation with her. While Delilah pulls the crème brulee from the oven so it can cool before setting it in the refrigerator, I sneak away to light the candles in the dining room. I never eat in here. This is for formal occasions and family dinners and there are never any of those at this house anymore. We do all the family things at Tommy and Jacelyn's since they have Jonah. It's easier.

"Okay, the kitchen is my favorite so far, but this room is a really close second," she says from the doorway behind me. "Question, though. If all the food is in the kitchen, and you have a big island with all those stools, why are we eating in here?"

This is why I needed my sister's advice. She would have told me this was overkill.

"It's too much?"

"A little. Don't get me wrong, I love it and you put a lot of thought into eating in here, but I'm not used to showy flashy houses, and people like that are kind of a turn off," she says. She kind of pulls the corner of her bottom lip in with her teeth and I wonder if I just messed it all up. "Maybe we can eat in here another night? Like if there's ever a date that involves your sister and her family."

"You want to have dinner with my sister and her whole crazy family?"

"You're part of that crazy family and I'm having dinner with you tonight, aren't I? What's a few more people. Just not tonight. Tonight, let's just keep it simple."

Delilah steps over to the table and slowly pulls a plate closer to her, tipping her head toward the door to the kitchen as she gathers the silverware in her other hand.

"C'mon. Simple. Let's get to know each other before we use the fabric napkins, okay?"

I smile, nod, and pick up the plate and flatware closest to me. Following her back into the kitchen, I make sure to blow the candles out on my way past.

Chapter 19

Delilah

He makes me feel soft.

When I was a kid, I felt like I needed to have rough edges to survive. Getting bounced from one home to another, sometimes feeling cared for and other times knowing I was just a monetary compensation, made it difficult to always be who I wanted to be. There were days I was able to be myself — but it was rare until Dan and Julie took me in. They made all the difference. That's why after all these years, even without them formally claiming me as their daughter, they're still my mom and dad.

When I was growing up with them during those later formative years, they instilled in me that softness was a good quality. The first several months, I would hide behind my hard exterior fearful the end of my living with them would come sooner rather than later. It didn't. Instead, Julie would pull me into the kitchen and say, "Come help me make cookies," and I would be surrounded by all her softness, all her love, and the hard exterior would naturally go away. Dan would sit reading books in a chair in the living room in the evening while I worked on finishing homework and he'd say, "Lilah, this book is amazing. You should read it," and I would. That is how I learned what love looks like.

There were times other kids would come in for respite care and those children were always looped right into the family, but I was the only permanent placement. They encouraged me to grow and step outside of my little box that held my security blanket and teddy bear and all the trauma I was spending time trying to hide from. Dan and Julie — Mom and Dad — helped shape me into the person I am. Sometimes that hard outer shell slides back over my shoulders like a comfortable blanket, but getting uncomfortable is how we grow.

Dinner with Fisher is making me uncomfortable in ways I never imagined. He's let me talk about me and my passions and my family. He hasn't pushed for information. He hasn't pushed away, either, not even when I explained to him about how my father was never in the picture and my mother's opioid addiction started out as back pain after a car accident when I was a toddler. He didn't offer me pity when he asked if I've tried to find her and I told him I knew exactly where she lives … Queen of All Saints Cemetery in Central Islip.

"I'm an orphan, Fisher."

"Orphans don't have families. You have Dan and Julie. There's Evelyn, who is basically a surrogate mom. You have me now, and with me you get Jacelyn, Tommy, Jonah, Brian and Stella and all their kids, and Stephanie and Max, and Mr. and Mrs. Barbieri, and Mama and Ben Stratford. I'll even throw in Caryn and Greg for good measure," he says, and I watch the emotion flood his face. "You're not without family."

The crème brulee has been chilled, sugared, torched, and eaten, and I'm slowly sipping a mug of Mexican hot chocolate while we sit at the island after dinner. The cocoa is a recipe Fisher's brother-in-law used to woo his sister, or so he says, but I'm sure there's more to that story. If I just keep drinking, he won't notice the tears, right? If I keep my head down, he won't see me brush them away.

"I was on the cusp of losing the family business," he says.

It's a tactic to draw the attention away from me and my situation. Tonight, we've gone beyond the limits of first dates. We have gotten comfortable with our pasts and torn the scabs off our wounds.

"Jacey was in college. I was trying to keep myself from ruining everything my parents worked for, and in the process started gambling. It was a stress reliever. A little here and there, then more. Then poker games and going to casinos to play Black Jack on the weekends. I was in so much debt, and the restaurant was starting to suffer because when you don't have the money to spend on quality products, you cut corners."

Lifting my head just enough to look at him, I forget my concerns about Fisher seeing me cry because I see the tears welling up in his eyes, too.

"Tommy walked in one night and said, 'This could be a really great restaurant.' I laughed at him because I was certain he was going to ask me if he could purchase it and lowball me on the assessed value. Instead, he gave me his card, and started working with me on marketing. Then he found out what I'd been doing … and he took me to gambling rehab. That's the short version. And now you and Tommy are the only two people who know something about me my own sister doesn't know."

I stare at him, curious where this is going and how our stories relate.

"Lilah," he says, savoring my name as he holds it on his lips, "I didn't have any family here when Tommy walked in that day. Jacey was still in California. I had Doris and the rest of the staff and people who had been coming in for years who knew my parents way back when, but I didn't have a family to call mine."

I see where he's going with this now, and I almost can't breathe. My chest is so tight, as if someone walked up behind me and tightened my corset way too much, and I might pass out. I try to quell the spinning and take a deep breath, opening my chest, and asking the universe to give me strength, because this man may be the one who gets me. Finally. I've never dated a person who understands how lonely it can be when you have no one who knows all your history.

"And after all you have been through there are all these people to support you."

"I was an orphan. I found my family. Jacelyn and I had no one — grandparents were all gone, Mom and Dad were both only children, we had literally no family." He reaches up and brushes the hair off my forehead, his fingertips trailing along my cheek until he gently lifts my chin. "You don't have to be an orphan either."

That's when I stop holding the tears in and let them run freely down my face. That's when he lifts his other hand and places it on my other cheek. When he slowly pulls me to him, I never want him to stop pulling me to him. Ever.

The first touch of his lips doesn't fall where I expect. He kisses one cheek, then the other, then finally he places them against mine. It isn't wanting, or demanding. It's careful and calculated as though he knows this is a fragile moment and doesn't want to break it. He doesn't want to break me.

I won't break.

I push against his mouth, tasting my tears on his lips, opening myself just enough to tell him I need more. I want more. I have never wanted more like I do right now.

*****

I do not drink coffee. Ever. I just never developed the taste for it.

This morning, I'm giving it another try. If I don't get myself woken up, I'll never survive my shift at work and then at Evie's baking tonight.

"What's in the cup?" Maggie pops the "p" on cup and I know she's digging for information. I never bring a morning beverage with me to work, so she's right to be suspicious. The thing is, I didn't tell her I was having dinner with Fisher last night, so I could potentially lie about why I'm so tired. She'd have to believe me.

One problem, though. I don't lie if I can help it. It's a bad habit to get into and just snowballs into oblivion. No, thank you.

"I decided to give coffee a chance. It's not as disgusting as I remember it being, but it could be because I added about nine packets of sugar and filled the mug halfway with milk," I say.

It's not a lie. I really did put that much crap in the cup. I just don't tell her Fisher made me try his cup of black coffee which is what prompted the need for so much extra.

"Gross," she says, wrinkling her nose. "You're going to be more wired and crash from the sugar than you would from any caffeine."

"Yeah, well I needed something to wake me up. It was a late night," I say.

I could hear a pin drop with how quiet the room is suddenly.

"I was business planning and trying to come up with a marketing strategy," I say.

Again, not a lie. After all the amazing kissing last night, Fisher and I did so much more talking. Honestly, I was surprised when we didn't run out of things to talk about between his family, my families, both our business aspirations, favorite foods, movies, places we want to visit. It's been so long since I cared to date anyone, I forgot how much I love learning about another human being. More than that, I think I really, truly enjoyed how much he was interested in learning about me. We lost track of time and forgot to sleep, which sounds insane, but we were still talking when the sun was coming up. I didn't go back to my apartment until the time I'm normally waking up in the morning, and that was only to shower and put on clean clothes for work.

"Must have been quite the brainstorm session," Maggie says, interrupting my thoughts. "I mean, you were working so hard you even have bruises from it."

Instinctively, I touch my neck. She starts laughing at me when I let out a low groan.

"I have makeup. It's not bad. We should be able to cover it up." She presses her lips together, and reaches into her bag for a small makeup kit. "You know you didn't have to fib."

"I wasn't fibbing. We really were talking about business stuff a lot of the night," I say, sheepishly. "Part of me doesn't want to get my hopes up that it's going to turn into more than a few dates. But, we both unpacked a lot of baggage last night and I just feel like he's someone I'm supposed to know."

Maggie walks over and wraps her arms around me. I should be used to the gesture from her by now, but I'm still surprised by it.

"Lilah, I just want you to be happy."

"I think he makes me happy," I say. "I'm generally a happy person, but I smiled so much last night. It was incredible."

I push aside the apprehension. It's still so new. It makes me nervous. A few weeks ago, I was ready to totally write him off as just another asshole. Worse, I tried to make him out to be some guy wanting to see me fail. Fisher doesn't want to see anyone fail, and it's amazing to have another person other than my foster parents and Evelyn lifting me up.

The bell ringing at the front counter pulls my attention back to work. I push through the swinging door ready to offer assistance to someone only to find a bouquet placed square in the center of the counter. Whoever delivered it is already gone, but tucked snuggly in the center of the sweet pea and lily arrangement is a card with my name on it. Pulling it out and flipping it over, the only thing written on the other side is, "Dinner tonight? —Fish."

The smile can't be wiped from my face. Maggie might have to pull me back down to reality for the rest of the day if I'm going to accomplish any work.

Chapter 20

Fisher

"You didn't sleep with her, did you?"

Rolling my eyes, I refill my coffee cup and walk away from Greg. I stuck around after Delilah left the coffeehouse, which I hadn't planned on doing. One of the local kids who works year-round for Brian and Greg called in sick, though, so I offered to stay and help until I need to head to the restaurant.

"You did, didn't you?" He follows me as I push through the doors to the kitchen. "You're the last one of us to find your person. It's been too long since one of us was single."

I stop short and turn around, nearly colliding with Greg and sloshing coffee over the edge of my mug.

"Okay, asshole. No. I didn't sleep with her," I say, under my breath. "I am not the kind of guy to pressure a woman, especially not on a first date. I'm going to take this slow. It's been a really long time since I even wanted to spend time with anyone other than this insane group of people I consider my family."

Staring at him, I wait for an apology.

"What?" he asks.

Why do I count him as family? He's like the annoying cousin who won't shut the fuck up. I don't even know why I told him I didn't sleep with her. Wait. No, that's not true. It's because if I hadn't answered him and he jumped to conclusions, it would have started a whole thing that involved Tommy and my sister. I don't need that.

"'What?'" I say, my tone mocking him as I turn back toward the ovens. "I really like her, man. She's got a past and she's got an amazing future ahead of her. Maybe, just maybe, I want to be part of her present."

Realizing he isn't following me across the room, I look over my shoulder to find him with a stupid grin on his face.

"You should write a romance novel with phrases like that."

I flip him the bird and continue on with my super important task of going into the office.

"When do you see her again?" he asks from the doorway.

"Hopefully tonight. I sent flowers to her with a card asking if she'd join me for dinner again." Twisting in the chair, I lean my head down on the desk and push my hands into my hair. What if she says no? And then, "We shared a lot of deep things, wounds we had and healing we've done. I don't want her to say no because I was a screw up for a long time."

"No one can say no to your beautiful face, Fish," Tommy says from behind Greg. He pokes his head through the door and smiles. "Chicks dig scars, even the emotional ones. Just look at your sister. Totally hooked up with this damaged guy and now she's tied down with a house and a baby."

This is why Tommy is one of my best friends and probably the only guy I ever would have been completely on board with my sister marrying. He's fun, but also a pretty serious person when it's needed. It looks like he's about to get serious with me as he nods his head toward the front of the coffeehouse and Greg steps out of the way to let him through. When the door closes, I feel my palms get a little clammy. Then he pulls up a plastic milk crate and sits on it, leaning up against the closed door.

"You were a screw up," he says, emphasizing the "were." "You've been on a good path for a handful of years and there's been zero reason for me to worry about you backsliding. How are things going?"

I shrug. I scrub my hand down the days' worth of stubble on my cheek and let out an exhausted breath.

"The business is good. I'm good. Bills are paid. It's not football or basketball season, so I don't have any temptation to place bets on anything. And when I came clean to you, I swore off casinos. I haven't stepped foot in one since that weekend," I say.

"No urges to go find your old bookie or hit the OTB?"

"None. I'm extra good," I say.

We play this game every once in a while where T does his dad routine on me and I make sure I'm honest because he's the only one I trust with this information. Well, he was the only one.

"And Delilah? I heard you say you two shared deep things, and I'm assuming you weren't talking with Greg about being intimate," he says, cocking an eyebrow.

I come clean and tell him everything I told her about my past. They're the only two who know.

"Do you miss it?"

"Miss what? The rush of wondering if I'm going to win? Sometimes, but I've got a nephew I want to see grow up and I much more prefer the kick of adrenaline I get from playing with him."

I don't need to be found in a gutter somewhere because I lost and owe the wrong person too much money. There were close calls when I was in deep. That was before I had people. It was before I had a family again.

"You want another one?"

"Another ... one? Another what?" I say, confused.

"Well, this one might not be a nephew, but I need to make sure you're in good form—"

"We're having another baby!?"

"Don't tell Jacelyn I told you yet," he says. Laughing, he adds, "Your face is priceless right now. You look like it's Christmas morning."

It might as well be. The funny thing is, I don't want to call and congratulate Jacey. I want to tell Delilah.

*****

I wait until early afternoon before I text her. I just want to know if she's up for dinner tonight, but what comes out is akin to me professing my undying love and falls just short of saying the "L" word. When I was typing it didn't sound bad. It was just very ... unmanly. The thing is, I don't regret it. After Jacey came back home from California, I decided life is way too damn short to hold back how I really feel with the people I care about.

My phone buzzes with a message and I smile seeing her name on the screen.

Delilah: I'm free tonight, especially after that massive outpouring of feelings. What were you thinking for food? I have a cake to bake when I get home so I can decorate tomorrow, but I could take a break and eat.

I think on it a minute. This is perfect. I'm at the restaurant until 7, so I could cook something for her here and take it to her at Evelyn's. I press the "call" button and lay out my plan for her.

"I was thinking," I say.

Before I can continue, she says, "Uh oh. That can't be good."

"Trust me, it's all good. Are you on board with a late dinner? I'm at the restaurant until seven-ish, but I'll cook and bring it to you at Evie's while you finish baking."

"Can't do that. I'm baking at my apartment," she says. "It's just a little cake."

That's a biggish step, going to her place.

"Are you prepared for me to see your apartment? Is that a thing you're okay with?" I ask.

She's quiet on the other end of the line and I start counting the seconds wondering if she's going to change her mind.

Eleven, twelve, thirteen …

"Why wouldn't I be okay with that?"

"I don't know, that's why I asked. Sometimes people like to keep their places private until they're more comfortable with the person they're dating," I say. I catch myself tripping over every other word as I try to choose them carefully.

"Is that what we're doing?"

I feel the hesitation in her voice more than I hear it and a brick settles in my chest. What if she doesn't do "dating?" Some women don't. Delilah doesn't strike me as a woman who would play the field.

"Do you want to be doing that? Dating, I mean."

What the hell else would I mean? I cringe a bit and slap my open hand to my forehead. Dumbass.

"I don't think I've ever actually dated anyone. Gone on a date, yes. Been dating as in a relationship? Not so much. I don't recall anyone getting past a third date with me, so … yeah," she says, shying away a bit in the end.

I bet she's blushing right now. She's so cute when her cheeks turn pink. I noticed last night when she was nervous, she started tugging on her right ear and playing with her earring. I want to date her and I'm going to get well beyond the third one.

"Well, I'm not sure why that is, but I'd like to break your streak of not dating."

"If that's the case, I suppose you can come to my apartment and feed me tonight," she says, playfully.

She gives me her address and tells me to surprise her, nothing is off limits.

"Raw oysters?"

"Ew. Okay, so there are a few things I won't eat," she says, only slightly disgusted.

"I'll see you tonight," I say when her laughter dies down.

"Tonight," she says. "I can't wait."

Chapter 21

SEPTEMBER
Delilah

He's gotten through the third date. He's even surpassed the fifth. For the sixth official date, we're getting together with his sister, Tommy, and Jonah.

Tomorrow night is the family dinner I told him I wanted and I'm nervous. So nervous I might actually vomit, because despite knowing Jacelyn and her family a little bit now it's still damn scary to meet the boyfriend's family in a formal setting. What if once we're in a meal situation I'm not the girl his little sister thinks her brother should be with? Maybe she'll think my past isn't something she wants her kids around, because I'm from the city and had a unique upbringing. Maybe she just won't like me and my past won't have anything to do with it. What if I'm just unlikeable?

"What are you thinking about?" he asks from across the table, reaching over to move my hair away from my face.

"How I might throw up," I deadpan.

Fisher's eyes go wide and he shifts in his chair. We haven't done anything that would make him concerned about me getting sick in the morning and he still looks nervous.

"What if Jacey doesn't like me?" I whine. "I don't want her to not like me, but I don't want to be awkward because I'm trying to be liked."

"What? She already loves you," he says, reaching across the table and cupping my face in his hand. "If I hear one more time how she's upset I've kept you from her for nearly two months, I might stop talking to her all together. It's kind of annoying."

Picking up my cocoa, I breathe in the rich chocolate scent. I like the way the warmth wraps around my tongue and heats me all the way through. It doesn't matter that it's September and hotter than I remember it ever being this time of year, I refuse to give in to the craze of frozen drinks that are meant to be warm.

"I'm glad she's confident, but what if she asks something about my childhood?" I ask while leaning into his touch.

"You be as honest with her as you want to be. If you don't want to answer a question or add to a conversation, don't. There is no wrong way to meet my sister," he says. "I mean, she was the one who told me I made you cry at the first event we did. She legitimately likes you more than she likes me and I share DNA with her."

That gets a smile out of me.

"I should get over to Evelyn's. I have a few orders for early next week to start working on and then baking tomorrow until I need to come to your house," I say.

Tipping my mug, I finish my drink and stand up. He remains seated. It's Friday and he doesn't go to the restaurant until closer to noon.

"Staying to help the guys again?"

"I like to gossip," he says, holding his arms out and shrugging.

"I'm sure you do. Don't talk about me too much, my ears ring every time you do."

I smile and bend to kiss him. He takes me by surprise and wraps an arm around my waist, pulling me onto his lap. We haven't done much more than make out and what Murph and Will would refer to as "heavy petting." It's not that we don't want to go further; I think he's just waiting for my cues. In the middle of his brother-in-law's brother's coffee shop is not the right time to give those cues.

Biting his lip, I pull him closer. There are more feelings here than I expected and I'm unsure what to do with them.

"Hey now. Maybe you two should get a room," Greg says as he strolls through picking up trash on a table near us. He laughs a little as he heads back toward the kitchen, and I'm sure he didn't mean anything rude by it, but I'm self-conscious with Fisher when we're in public. Everyone knows him. No one knows who I am.

Or it feels that way.

Some days, I still feel like I'm just the cake lady.

Fisher touches my face again and I breathe into him, relaxing my body against his.

"Where did you go?" he asks.

I hear the concern in his voice before I open my eyes to look at him. Meeting his gaze, I see the worry.

"Nowhere," I whisper. "I've just never had someone be affectionate in public with me like you are. It sometimes makes me feel insecure."

"How?"

"Like I don't belong here, doing this, with you."

"I'm in love with you, Delilah. I never want you to feel like this is just for show, because it's not."

"You're —," I stop talking. I try to process. I can't. He just said that, didn't he?

"I am. I know it's probably too soon by someone's standards, but I've felt more since meeting you than I have in a long time. I like feeling."

Smiling, I place my lips against his again, and mumble, "I like feeling, too."

*****

It was so difficult to pry myself away from Fisher this morning, but I needed to get started on the cake designs for a new customer. Business has grown exponentially since I started letting people know I'm pursuing this as a real career. My dream was never to be a grocery store baker, I just don't have the confidence yet to quit my day job. So, I split my time between the store and Evelyn's.

And Fisher. He's taking more of my time than I've allowed anyone else in a long time.

"Maybe you should consider cutting back on your hours at the grocery," Evie says as though she's reading my thoughts.

Seated at the counter across from me, the light streaming in through the open door gives her an angelic glow. The windows lining the east side of the dining room allow the sun to heat the front of the house on cooler days and offer ample natural light to bring out the beauty of original hardwood floors and exposed beams. It makes me think of yellows and oranges. In turn, those remind me of the warmth I feel when Fisher hugs me, when I talk to Genevieve on the phone about simple things, and when I write a quick note to my mom.

"Maybe."

She picks up her coffee cup, her hands temporarily stained brown from digging in the dirt and her nails cut to the quick to keep from ripping them while working with the horses.

"What's holding you back?"

She slowly sips her coffee, waiting for my response. I slowly sketch a swirl pattern in my notebook, waiting to find my brave. I have no reason to not share with her, but something feels so intimate about it despite all we've shared in the past.

She sets her cup down and, through the hair that's fallen in my face I see her stare at her hands.

"When I was fifteen, I got pregnant," she says following a deep breath.

I haven't heard this story. My pencil stops moving. My ears are ready to listen.

"My parents were livid. Then they weren't. Then they were scared," she says, placing her thumbs and forefingers together to make a diamond shape on the counter. "I was dating a boy who was a little older than me. He had a car and his parents had money."

"Did you … " I can't even finish the sentence. I've watched Dirty Dancing enough times to know what money can buy when you're in an unwanted situation.

"No. Heaven's no. I would never be able to do something like that, and if I did my parents would have disowned me. They came to the decision they were okay with me having the baby, but I was only a child myself," she says, lost in a memory. "Neither of us were ready to try to raise a baby. His parents helped us and we found a couple who wanted to adopt. Not because they couldn't have their own kids. They had two biological children already, but they wanted more and fell in love with my baby the moment they laid eyes on her."

I'm waiting patiently for the bomb to drop. There has to be a moral to the story. There's always a lesson, isn't there?

"I held back from signing the paperwork. I needed to be sure I was making the right decision. The thing is, as soon as I met them, I knew they were the people I wanted to have raise my child. The fear of the unknown kept me from going through with it immediately. When she was four days old, I finally said enough was enough," she says. We look at one another for the first time since she started talking. "Sometimes, you have to trust you're making the right decision even if it feels like the hardest thing you've ever done."

Evelyn wipes the tears off her cheeks, finishes her coffee, and smiles at me.

"What's holding you back?"

"What if I fail?"

"What if you don't?" she counters. She watches me, waiting for me to say something. When I don't, she asks me again, "What is holding you back?"

"Nothing," I say, without a second thought. "Absolutely nothing."

She smiles through fresh tears and stands up,

My mind begins to wander as she comes around the counter, places her coffee cup in the sink, and wraps her arm around my shoulder. Placing a barely there kiss against my temple, she says, "Atta girl. Take this town by storm. Make them wonder why you hid your famous fondant from them for so long. You're going to have so much business you'll have to hire two more of you."

I pay attention as she walks out the side door to the parking area and wonder what it must have really been like for her to give up a child. I can see how much it still hurts. The math tells me I'm around the age her daughter would be now, and it starts to make sense. I start to learn the lesson. We were meant to find one another. All along, she was meant to be part of my surrogate family just like Fisher said.

The vibrating in my dress pocket pulls my attention back and I lift my phone up to see a new message from Maggie.

Mags: I'm bored and out of work early. Where are you?

Swiping my finger across the screen, I reply quickly so I can attempt to get back to work.

Me: Evelyn's working on designs for a new customer. Come help.

I hesitate before sending it when I hear Evie's voice ask me again what's holding me back.

"Send. Time to quit being scared of your own shadow, Lilah."

*****

"Oh my God, this is so exciting!" she squeals.

I recoil a bit from the shrieking, but smile at Maggie anyway ... because it is exciting.

"So, are you going to cut back on hours, or just put in your notice?"

"I'm going to start with asking to cut back on my hours. The less I'm there, the more I can focus here."

"I'll miss you when you quit, you know. I'm probably going to be a lifer like Mike," she says.

When she showed up, there really wasn't anything I needed help with. After my conversation with Evie, though, I didn't exactly want to be alone with my thoughts. They were starting to wander toward dangerous territory, namely in the direction of the "Why was Delilah unadoptable?" terrain.

She cuts the tip off a new piping bag and the hole is nearly microscopic. She's just playing around, but while I pull ingredients out for cake, I pay close attention to her.

Parchment paper. Melted chocolate. Piping bag.

Then she slowly swirls the chocolate over the paper in an intricate design that looks oddly familiar.

I don't let on that I'm watching her and instead carry on the conversation as I begin measuring and mixing.

"What makes you think you'll be there forever?"

"I'm local, born and raised, and have no money to go to college. It doesn't help that I'm thirty years old and live at home. Plus, I'm not sure I know what I want to be when I grow up anyway, so I just hold on to mediocrity at the grocery store, occasionally have adultish beverages with other wannabe adults, and wonder why it's taken New York so long to legalize weed," she says, never breaking her concentration as she moves her arm around above the parchment. "Aaaaaaand done."

"That's gorgeous, Mags."

"Thanks. It's your design."

Say what? I've never drawn anything like that in my life, I think to myself. Then, she holds up my sketchbook and there it is. The doodling from when I was talking to Evelyn.

"I mean, it's not exact or perfect, but pretty close. It's easier if I have the paper on top of the drawing, but," she shrugs.

"Why don't you ever do anything like that at work?" I ask, but I already know the answer.

"They don't pay me barely livable wages to be creative."

What's holding you back, Lilah?

I smile at her, "What if … what if you had the opportunity to do something like that all the time? Would you take it?"

"Absolutely," she says, no hesitation. "You have thoughts, don't you?"

"I do. I have many thoughts. First, I need to trim back my hours and make sure it'll all work," I say. "I know I'm going way out on a limb and I'm not usually one to do that, but if everything falls into place do you want to work with me?"

She hums a little like she's thinking it over while attempting to hide a smile.

"Fucking duh. Of course, I'm in," she says.

"I can't promise everyone will want chocolate designs, but I know you have way more talent than that up your sleeve."

"Oh, yeah, I do." The smile on her face tells me I'm making the right decision following my gut. When the smile falters, I worry she's already having second thoughts, but Maggie surprises me when she says, "Thank you for taking a chance on me and giving me an outlet. I'm really glad I messaged you today and came to hang out."

I smile, tell her I'm happy she came out, too, and flip the mixer on. It's time to go to work.

Chapter 22

Fisher

Telling Delilah I'm in love with her was not planned. In fact, I was pretty sure I wasn't going to tell her that until at least the two-month mark, but here we are. She didn't say it back and that's okay. When she's ready to she will. I hope.

"What if she doesn't say it back?"

Jacelyn, Tommy, and Jonah came over to the house early so I could have some extra uncle time before dinner. Naturally, before the charcuterie board is even started, she's grilling me about my relationship.

"What do you mean?" Tommy asks. "She'll say it back, just give her time. This is still so new and she has a lot going on. You came into the picture right when she was starting her own thing."

"I was just starting my own thing, too, though," I say a bit defensively.

Jacey rolls her eyes at me and I shoot her a "what?" look.

"I know, but you already have a ton of experience doing this stuff. She's out there at the bottom," Jacey says.

I nod, staring down into my beer. It's true, Delilah and I met at that first event, and she seemed super confident in herself but I know it's been difficult for her to really get going between still working full time and trying to work out of her tiny apartment. I thought she was exaggerating when she told me how small it was, and then I actually saw it for the first time. She told me she downsized in an attempt to save money, but regretted it almost immediately.

"She's pretty amazing, you know?" I say rhetorically. "You think she'll say it back?"

"I'm pretty confident she will, but just play it by ear, Fish."

Tommy barely finishes the statement when I hear a light knock at the kitchen door. The knob turns and Delilah pokes her head through gracing us all with a smile that lights up the room. She makes everything feel brighter, the difficult moments less dark. Our eyes meet and I return the smile, welcoming her with a gentle kiss on the lips.

"Hi. You taste like cake," I say. "You got done earlier than you expected?"

"I did. Maggie's helping me, so things were moving a little quicker this morning," she says, handing her bag to me so I can hang it on her hook in the laundry room off the kitchen. "I might have taste tested a small cupcake. I was playing with almond flour and I'm trying to decide if I like the way it works."

"I'm sure it's amazing," I say, tasting her again. "Come on in and make yourself comfortable. Food's pretty much ready so we can eat whenever."

She scoots past me and immediately kneels down to strike up a conversation with the smallest person in the room. For a kid who is usually a little leery of new people, Jonah seems to warm up to her without hesitation. I watch for a second and then turn to put her bag away.

"He's really taking to you," I hear Jacelyn say, surprised.

"Does he not usually like new people?"

As I walk out of the laundry room, Tommy smiles at me and Jacey laughs.

"No not at all. He's got his favorite people and is pretty cautious around everyone else," my sister says.

"I never would have known," Delilah says. "When I was a kid, I was ignored a lot by adults, so I try to make sure I address the littlest ones first so they know they're important, too."

"Fisher, I think I love her, too," Jacey blurts out.

We all laugh, and I realize if there was going to be any awkward tension tonight, it disappears instantaneously.

*****

"You did not," Jacey says.

"I did. It wasn't the first time I ran away, either," Delilah says, picking up her glass of water and taking a sip. "I ran away from every home except for Dan and Julie's. It's sad, really, because I always went to the same place so as soon as it was reported the social worker would come find me sitting at the nearest bus stop."

We're all glued to her. She was so worried her past would taint any possible conversation with my sister, but instead I'm seeing my mom come out of Jacey more than ever.

"Where were you going?"

"That's the thing. I have no idea. I was so little, you know. My mother had told me my father was from White Plains, so part of me planned to find my way there, but I had no idea where that even was or if the city bus could get me there," she says. "By the time I got to Dan and Julie, I had figured out how to get to White Plains if I wanted to run away again. It was never a need. I was extremely fortunate. No one ever hurt me, but it didn't mean I wasn't careful how much I shared."

She's quiet for a moment and I think we all see it. The fear she used to feel is hidden under her mask of bravery and it slips just a little.

"Mom and Dad never made me feel like I wasn't wanted, though. I wish they would have adopted me, but it wasn't meant to be," she says. Her phone starts vibrating on the table beside her and she looks at it, perplexed. "Excuse me a minute."

Delilah leaves the table in the dining room and quietly answers her phone as she walks back into the kitchen.

"Are you okay?" I hear her ask.

"Well, I guess I need to start planning a wedding because I want her in the family," Jacelyn says.

"Yeah, you should," I respond, but I was hardly listening so I'm not entirely sure what I'm agreeing to. Watching the kitchen door, I wonder if I should check on her or if I should just stay sitting here with Jonah on my lap and wait patiently.

"I want more nieces and nephews ASAP, too," Tommy adds. "You should get started tonight."

"Huh?" I ask, and I'm sure the look I give him is straight up fear. "We haven't even done that yet."

"Good for you," my sister says.

"Really?" Tommy counters.

"I sense some tension. Perhaps you two need it more than we do?"

"Nah, we're good. Remember? I got her pregnant again. We have plenty of sex," Tommy says.

Jacelyn can barely contain herself, laughter bubbling over. I forgot how much I love hearing my sister laugh and enjoy life.

"You two are insane."

"True, but we both really like her and think this is a good thing. We should do more date nights together. Maybe next time go out and leave Jonah with Mama and Ben for the night," Jacelyn says, hopeful.

"That sounds —," I begin as Delilah comes back into the room. "What's wrong?"

Her face looks ashen against the fire red of her hair.

"A lot. I need to go to Long Island," she says. "Right now."

"I'll grab a bag. We'll stop at your place to get your things," I say, no questions asked. I always have a bag ready to go if I need it, because you just never know.

"No, you don't have to do that. I'll be fine," she says, but I can see the weight of concern beginning to build up on her shoulders.

Jacey and I exchange a look. She's telling me to go.

"I do. Two minutes and we're out of here," I say.

Chapter 23

Delilah

I ruined our evening with Jacey and Tommy. That's what's going through my head as I throw underwear, a dress, shorts and shirts, and my toothbrush into my backpack. Fisher hasn't even asked what's going on. He just threw his bag in his car, opened the door for me, brought me home, and is insistent on driving me to Long Island.

"I think that's all I need," I say coming out from the bedroom and catching him holding a picture of me, Genevieve, and Jax from my trip down to meet them.

"They look like they belong to you," he says, catching me off guard.

"I feel like they should," I say without a second thought.

He sets the photo back on the shelf and opens the door for me. The address is already in his GPS, so it's just a matter of driving until we need gas.

"Are you sure you're okay to drive? You had a beer earlier," I say.

It was hours ago. It was one drink. He's eaten plenty since then. I just worry.

"I'm perfect, but if you'd like to drive the first leg to be sure I'll allow it," he says in a playful tone.

"I trust you." Hearing his words roll through my head again, I smile a bit. For a guy who was such an asshole a few months ago, he is kind of perfect. But I'm not going to tell him that right now. Now is the time to wait for updates on Dan's condition.

The silence between us is comfortable, the music from the radio filling whatever void there might have been. We're miles from home when he finally asks.

"Do you want to talk about it?"

Looking at my hands, I study my unpainted nails. The pink dye catches my eye where it has stained my finger tips from working this morning on projects that are thankfully completed and just need to be delivered or picked up. Maggie can handle it. I won't cry.

"Dan was shot during a carjacking. I don't know where it happened or where he was hit, but he wasn't dead. When Mom called, she was on the way to meet the ambulance at the hospital so I don't know more than that really," I say. "I'm waiting for her to call and tell me what's happening."

"Who's with the kids?" he asks.

Fisher is levelheaded and if he's anything like I think he is, his first thought is Dan will be in good hands. His second is Genevieve and Jax and that ... that means so much more to me than if he asked questions about Dan that I don't have answers to.

"Another family close by. They're waiting for me to get there," I say.

I haven't told him yet that both their parents' rights were terminated after being absent for nearly the entire time they've been in foster care. It didn't matter how many times they skipped visitations or court dates, something always got messed up in the paperwork to keep them from being listed for adoption. Those babies have been without a real family for long enough. Their parents never even came to court and Gen said she hasn't heard anything from either of them since before they were placed with Dan and Julie. Now might not be the time to tell him I'm in the process of adopting them, or trying anyway. The one-bedroom apartment might set any progress back a little.

"Good. I'm glad they're safe. Are we going straight to them or the hospital first?"

"To them. Mom will let me know when to come to the hospital. Since I'm not technically their daughter, I don't know how that'll work if he ends up in ICU," I say.

I begin to lose interest in my hands and look at his profile in the dark, lit up only by the lighting on the GPS screen. We still have a lot of hours left to travel. Our relationship is still so new, and this feels like a huge jump. Both feet first into the deep end huge.

Father Murphy told me last week to trust my gut, let my instinct lead a little. He was right when he told me something similar about Fisher and about getting close with Genevieve and Jax. So, I close my eyes and try to figure out what my gut is telling me, and I feel my stomach sour.

"What if he doesn't make it, Fisher? What happens if I don't get to see him again?"

He reaches across the center console and takes my hand in his, intertwining our fingers and hugging them into his warmth as best he can.

"Then we figure out how long you need to be in Long Island to help Julie. But before worrying about that, let's get there. Right now, the most important thing is he got to the hospital in time."

We're quiet for a few more minutes when my phone buzzes in the cup holder.

Mom: In surgery now. Call when you can.

I press the call button and listen as the line connects.

"Mom? How bad is it?"

"I'm not entirely sure yet. He just went back. It looks like he was shot in the side and his left leg, so they're moving as quickly as they can."

"Is it close to his spine?"

"It is. We won't know how bad it is until after he's done in surgery. Now is the time to call in any favors to your angels, Lilah," she says. I hear her voice crack as she continues, "I can't lose him. He's my entire life. I've loved him since I was fourteen."

All I can offer her is a weak, "I know, Mom," before I can't hold my tears back any longer and we cry together. There is so much uncertainty and for the moment we only have each other to cling to.

Fisher squeezes my hand, a little added assurance that he's still there as we hurry as fast as we can to get to the only people I've ever let get close enough to me to love.

*****

"Lilah, wake up. We're here," I hear whispered through the fog of a dissipating dream.

Opening my eyes slowly, Fisher gives me a weak smile. I must have fallen asleep at some point, but I don't remember the last road sign I saw. I had to have been asleep for two or three hours.

"We're here. I'm not sure where here is, but it's the address you put in the GPS, so I assume it's where we're supposed to be," he says.

The porch light is the only one on at the tan house in front of me. I'm unfamiliar with the family Julie was able to send the kids to, and I freeze.

"Let's go get your kids," Fisher says, and it instantly makes me move.

I'm barely out of the car when a light turns on inside and the front door flies open. They rush to me and I wrap them up in my arms like I'm never going to let go.

"Hi babies. Are you okay?" I say, pulling Jax closer and kissing the top of his head.

I touch his face so he'll look up at me. As his eyes reach mine, he pulls me down to his level and throws his arms around my neck.

"Thank you for coming for us," he says against my skin.

Genevieve wraps her arms around us and hugs tightly.

Glancing up at the porch, I see a young woman and man standing there witnessing our moment. I hardly pay attention when Fisher walks past me and up the steps, holding his hand out to the couple. The conversation doesn't matter, I don't care what small talk they have, as long as I don't have to be the one having it.

"How is Dan?" the woman asks Fisher.

"Last we heard he was in surgery, but that was a couple hours ago."

"Let Julie know we're thinking of them when you talk to her," the man says, his voice aching with sincerity. "I was one of their fosters for a short time when I was about Genevieve's age. Dan was a huge influence on me and I just can't believe something like this has happened to such a good guy."

That catches my attention and I stare at him, taking in all the features and the way he stands. No way. It can't be.

"Davey?" I say a little louder than I anticipated.

He turns his head to look at me and I watch a huge, playful smile form. "No one has called me that in years, Liler."

"Oh my God." My heart stops. I return his smile. "I always wondered where you went."

The kids and I separate from our big hug, and as a group walk over to the porch. Davey comes down the stairs and, at first, he seems unsure of how to respond to seeing me after all these years.

"Let's not make it weird, okay?" he asks, opening his arms to me. I give him a hug that rivals the one I gave Gen and Jax. "It's so good to see someone from the old days. What are you doing? Where did you end up after I left?"

Sighing deeply, pressing my cheek into his shoulder, I say, "I never got to leave."

He pushes me back and looks at me, surprised. "She never came back for you?"

"Nope. I think she wanted to, but you know how it works. Then, things happened and she was just gone one day, forever. Dan and Julie kept me. I aged out, went to college with their help, and now I'm living upstate."

"It's not really upstate. It's called Western New York," Fisher says from the porch.

"Yeah, yeah, I hear that all the time," I say without looking at him.

Davey and I smile at each other again and he turns, hooking his arm through mine so we can walk together up the porch steps.

"Upstate, eh? It's a long way from home. Do you get back here often?"

"Not as much as I would like to."

"Maybe once we get Dan back home, we can have a family reunion," he says. "He's going to pull through. I can feel it."

He always was the positive one. When we were kids, I worked really hard to remain positive because if I didn't, Davey would call me out for it.

"I hope you're right. I don't think we can lose him without losing Mom, too," I say, emotion flooding my voice. "He is all she's ever known. Well, him and all of us throughout the years."

"If that happens — and that's a huge if — we'll hold her together like they did for us, Liler. We'll have to," he says.

I nod. Discussion over.

Davey and I talk about what we've both been up to all these years while his wife and Fisher make idle chit chat. It feels like we talk forever, but it isn't long enough before my phone rings in my dress pocket.

"Mom? How is he?"

I nod my head but no one else can hear her end of the conversation. I stare at Fisher. He tilts his head asking all the silent questions.

"Is he in recovery? Do they have any idea if he'll be paralyzed?"

Yes, in recovery. No, they aren't sure yet what his mobility will be like.

"But he's alive, Lilah. He's still here," she says, weeping on the other end of the phone. "He's still with us."

"Do you want us to come to the hospital?"

"Wait until morning. He'll be going up to ICU at some point, so let's get him in a room first. Are you with the kids yet or still driving?"

"Okay, we'll wait. We're at Davey's with the kids. This was a nice surprise considering the circumstances," I say. "You hadn't said who Gen and Jax were staying with."

She didn't even think about it. After Davey left the house, he kept in touch with her and Dan. When he grew up, he and his wife moved in just a few blocks away.

"They became respite providers and when I got the call about Danny, he was my first call so I could make sure the kids were somewhere safe until you could get here," she explains even though she doesn't need to. I hear a muffled voice in the background and Julie says, "Lilah, I'm going to let you go. The doctor just came out again. There are cheesy potatoes and leftover pork steaks in the fridge in case you're hungry when you get to the house. It's late, but try to get some rest. I love you."

"Love you, too."

I push the phone back into my pocket and am met with five pairs of eyes waiting for an update.

"He's in recovery, not sure about paralysis yet, he's going to ICU, there's pork and potatoes in the fridge, and she loves you."

"Cheesy or mashed?" Jax asks.

"Cheesy." I can't help smirking. I love this kid so much already.

"ICU? Will we be able to see him?" Gen asks.

"I don't know, sweetheart. Once he's up there, I'll ask, but I do know there's an age restriction sometimes."

She nods, wrapping her arms around my waist and making herself small against me. I brush her hair back and notice for the first time there's a reddish tint to the chestnut brown that wasn't there before.

"Did you dye your hair?"

"Julie helped me. I was hoping it would help convince the judge to let us be a family if I looked more like you," she says.

Oh, my heart cannot handle this right now. Then I catch Fisher's puzzled look. I offer a meek smile, and send up a prayer that he waits until the kids are back at the house and in bed before the conversation happens. I know it has to happen now, and yet we're still so new. I don't have time to worry about his reaction.

"Liler, I would love to visit longer, but these kids are starting to fade fast and need some rest," Davey says. He breaks my concentration and pulls me away from the incoming emotional overload. Ruffling Jax's hair when he catches him yawning, he says, "How about brunch tomorrow? We'll bring food to you guys at the house before you go to the hospital?"

I nod and say it sounds like a good plan, but at this point anything I don't have to decide is good. Fisher shakes Davey's hand and thanks him again for keeping the kids "for us" until we could get here.

"It's no problem. Dan and Julie were able to pull me from a rough situation and get me on the right path. I owe them a lot. I'd do anything for them."

Without hesitation, Fisher wraps an arm around Davey and pats him on the back in half-hug.

"We'll see y'all in the morning then."

Fisher reaches his hand out and Jax takes it. They walk to the car and I watch as my brand new boyfriend helps get my maybe, almost, could be mine soon son into the seat and makes sure he's buckled.

It's all too much and Davey can see it before I even make a move. He steps up to me again, placing his hands on my shoulders and his forehead against mine.

"It's going to be okay. I don't know how long you two have been seeing one another, but whatever it is you're freaking out about right now, don't. He doesn't know you're in the process of adopting them, does he?"

I shake my head and whisper, "No. We've only been together a few weeks. I haven't told him much about the kids."

"I think it's time to air the dirty laundry. No reason to start your relationship without being one hundred percent honest. Right?"

"Right," I say, closing my eyes and taking a deep breath. "I didn't think I missed anyone from the old days until I saw you tonight. People think they get it, but unless they were living our childhoods, they have such a limited view."

"I know. I live with one everyday who had a different upbringing. It's okay, though. We all grow and learn from one another. We all have a closet full of shit we want to forget about."

Chapter 24

Fisher

"Lilah's going to be our new mom," Jax says as I buckle him in.

"I kind of got the impression that was the plan," I say.

I can't say I was at all prepared to hear Genevieve say what she said about her hair. There's no way I could be when none of our conversations have veered toward having kids. The picture of the three of them in her apartment looks like a little family, and I even told her they look like they belong together, but it's a little different when it's confirmed. Not in a bad way, just in a "that discussion hasn't happened" way. Delilah hasn't said a thing about having children let alone adopting a bunch of kids from Long Island, only that they're foster kids staying with the couple who raised her.

The rear passenger door opens and Genevieve climbs up into the seat beside her brother unaware of the conversation he just started. Maybe it's a conversation I should stop and have first with Delilah.

"If she's our new mom and you fall in love with her, are you going to be our new dad?"

"Jaxson!" Genevieve scolds, but I'm not even phased by the question at this point. I try to adapt quickly, and I'm learning with this new relationship that knowing how to switch gears is a good talent to have.

"It's okay. It's a valid question," I say, lifting my hand to quell the hysteria. "The thing is, guys, I'm pretty sure I'm already in love with her, so the rest would be up to Delilah. Maybe for tonight, though, we can just worry about food, sleep, and making sure Dan is on the mend? Yeah?"

"Yeah," they say in unison.

"Awesome," I say backing out of the back door of the car. "Because I could really use some pancakes. You guys like pancakes?"

The kids look at each other and then back at me.

"Who doesn't like pancakes?" Jax asks.

I shrug and say, "No idea, but I'm glad it isn't you. I'll grab Delilah and we'll head over."

Closing the door, I look back to where Delilah and Davey are standing with their foreheads together. It scares me the way the jealousy bubbles up so quickly. It's jealousy and an animal instinct to pull her away from him. I feel my jaw clench before I see his wife on the porch locked onto him with a death glare of her own.

His wife.

Delilah and Davey shared a family when they were kids without families. I don't think they've seen each other since, and that's a lot to take in after spending hours in the car.

I feel the jealousy shift with the realization that I've stood with my own sister the same way during a heart-to-heart once or twice. I don't know what their marriage is like, but his wife can have all the feelings she wants to have about the scene before us. Taking a step in their direction, I quietly say her name and she turns her head at my voice.

All I see is love. I would say it doesn't matter that she didn't say it back, but I really want her to. I'll wait to hear the words, but right now the look in her eyes says it for her.

"Are you about ready to head out? The kids are beyond tired and we could use some rest, too."

She nods, pulls Davey in for another quick hug, and then steps away.

"I'll text you in the morning about brunch. Julie made sure I had your number," he says.

"Thanks, for everything. We'll see you tomorrow," Delilah says, lifting her hand in a small wave toward the porch. Davey's wife reciprocates, the ice melting a bit from her gaze as Delilah reaches for my hand and we turn toward the car.

"Everything okay?" I ask, not really expecting an honest answer. I never do when I ask a generic question like that no matter who I'm asking. Everyone always says things are fine, anyway.

"Mostly. It's just a lot to take in," she says. Releasing my hand, Delilah meanders to the passenger side, opens the door, and climbs up into her spot. I assumed that would be the end of the conversation, but once she's buckled and putting the next address into the GPS, she says, "Davey and I spent about a year in the house together when we were Gen's age. His aunt and uncle were able to take him after that and I don't remember hearing from him much after that. Between Dan in the hospital and seeing Davey, it really hits hard how much I've taken some people for granted."

I look at her skeptically as I finish backing out of the driveway. Putting the car into drive, I take the bait ... even if it wasn't supposed to be bait.

"For granted? How so?"

"Well, you know how I feel about family. I don't have one. Then you come into my life, stir things up, tell me about all these people who are family even if they aren't blood, and now here we are, hardly together two months, driving around Long Island picking up kids you don't know and meeting my long, lost foster brother." She's practically out of breath when she finishes and I glance at her when I make the next right turn. "You had a normal childhood, Fisher. My childhood was spent wondering if I'd get to go home again even though I didn't want to go back to that home in particular. I just wanted a place that *was* home. I took all these people here for granted and not once has Julie or Dan turned their back on me in all these years, but I want to get sad because I never got adopted. Now, Davey pops up and he's right there in my corner, too, because he understands what it was like to be a kid without a permanent place for a while. His wife is like you. Had normal."

"Whoa, Lilah. There are a lot of different versions of normal and it all depends on who you talk to," I say. Then I realize I called her "Lilah," which I haven't done. Ever. I try not to get stuck on that fact and continue, but what the fuck was I saying?

"I like when you call me Lilah," she says quietly and reaches for my hand in the dark. "I just want to have normal. I want to know what that's like. To have family I can rely on and Sunday picnics and a sister to argue with about something stupid."

"You know, that's not normal for everyone, right? You're talking about the white picket fence life, and it doesn't always exist. I'll make it happen for you, but just know that's not what works for everyone."

I feel her grip squeeze and release slightly.

Glancing in the mirror I see both Genevieve and Jax are sound asleep, so I take a chance.

"Once these little people are yours, what do you want your normal to look like?"

"Teaching them how to be loved the way she should have loved them. I want them to know they're a priority. Family dinners and weekend breakfast adventures," she says. "You caught on quickly."

"It was difficult not to catch on to your plans when Jax told me you were going to be their new mom," I say, a smile on my face. I won't tell her the rest. That's for me.

She covers her mouth with her free hand.

"Oh man. I should have talked to you about this way before now. You shouldn't find out you're dating a wannabe single mom from her soon-to-be kids."

I laugh. How can I not laugh? She's adorable, from the top of her fiery red head to the tips of her Converse All Stars, and I love everything about her.

"Total transparency. That weekend I came down here, the weekend we decided to call our truce, was the first time I met the kids. They took my heart, Fisher. They've been through a lot and Julie and Dan's house was their first permanent placement. I want it to be their last, too. They deserve a childhood free of fear that someone isn't going to keep them forever," she says.

I nod, though I don't know if she sees me.

"Forever sounds like a good deal," I say as I signal and turn at the destination the GPS says I've arrived at. Putting the car in park, Delilah and I take a deep breath and let it out at the same time. "I love the way you are giving yourself to them. They don't just deserve a good childhood. They deserve you as a mom because you love with everything in your soul, and that's something they need more than breakfast adventures and family dinners."

She unbuckles, but instead of reaching for the handle she pushes up and crosses the invisible line between us. I feel her hand on my cheek in the darkness, the only light in the car coming from the garage in front of us. Her lips find mine like they're magnetized and she places the gentlest kiss against my mouth.

"I've decided," she says when she pulls away.

"Decided what?" My brow furrows with the question.

"That I love you, too."

Without another word, she slips out the door and up to the house, keys in hand.

Chapter 25

Delilah

"They won't let the kids in because they're not old enough. They won't let you in because you're not family. They're making an exception for me as his daughter," I rattle off as I end my call with Julie.

Dan was sent up to ICU after surgery. The bullet in his leg went directly through and left him with muscle damage and flesh wounds. The surgeon was able to put him back together without any issues. The one closer to his spine, not so much. It fragmented when it hit bone and shattered some of his vertebrae. There are a lot of questions and no answers yet.

Julie is hopeful Dan will be moved to a regular floor later today if everything goes well, but that's a huge "if" as so much is still up in the air. I'm not counting on it. I also don't want to wait any longer to see him. I need to see him.

I look at Fisher and hope he'll tell me what decision I need to make. I haven't asked him for his opinion, but the questions are hanging in the air.

"Do you want me and the kids to take you to the hospital? We could drop you off and sit in the waiting room. I'm sure they have board games or something in there," he says.

We both glance at the children sitting at the kitchen table with us. Davey hasn't arrived yet, so I have no input from him. I don't have to have his input, though, because as much as we were close as kids, Dan and Julie raised me for half my life before I was considered an adult. He was here for a short time by comparison. Even if he's stayed in touch all these years, they are still my parents.

"Or the kids and I can go get milkshakes at this diner I found near the hospital and wander around for a bit. They can show me their stomping grounds," he says, winking at Jax. "There's got to be a playground near here."

"Or both?" I suggest. "Milkshakes, playground, and then come back and hang in the waiting room for a bit."

Genevieve and Jaxson both nod their heads vigorously. Settled.

A knock at the kitchen door shifts our attention just as Davey turns the knob and pops his head in.

"Good morning!" he calls, stepping through and greeting us all with a box from the local bakery. "I wasn't sure what everyone would be in the mood for so there's a lot. Um … yeah, let's just go with that."

The morning is easy. We attempt light conversation, Jax pulls Fisher around the house showing him his artwork from school, and Genevieve sits quietly reading a book. We wait a bit longer for Mom to call me back to let me know the plan before putting food away and heading toward the hospital.

*****

"Text me if you need us to come back sooner. I'm going to try to keep them occupied for a couple hours at least. If I don't hear from you first, I'll text when we're heading back," he says. I've hardly paid attention. I just innately trust him with Gen and Jax. When he lifts my chin to lock eyes with me, I wonder if I missed something more important than the scheduling. "Sound good?"

I nod slightly, dipping my chin against his hand before tipping my head to kiss his palm.

"Sounds great. I think a couple hours out and about will do them good," I say. "Just be sure to use GPS on your phone if you get lost."

"You don't trust my internal compass?" he questions, covering his heart with a hand and feigning hurt. A smile changes his features and he continues, saying, "Yeah, I don't trust it either. Get inside. We'll see you in a bit."

When he leans in to kiss me, we whisper to one another at the same time, "I love you." A quick smile, a few more hasty hugs and kisses on the tops of the kids' heads, and I slip through the entrance to the hospital.

The elevator ride to the Intensive Care Unit gives me almost too much time to think. My heart is breaking because of the reason we're here, but this little trip he forced himself to take with me is bringing out all the feelings. I tend to hide behind my hair and usually quiet demeanor, my earbuds in and my head in the clouds. He doesn't make me feel like I need to do that. He brings out the loud in me — all the loud things from my voice to my clothes. Everything is more colorful with him. And because of that, I think I'm handling the heartbreak about what happened to Dan a lot better.

I step from the car and Julie is waiting for me at the elevator bank.

"Lilah," she says, and opens her arms wide.

"Mom. How is he?" As we cling to one another, I feel the slightest tremor as it works its way through her. The strong shoulders that held me up through countless nights, always wondering if my mother would ever come back, begin to quake and I just let her collapse against me.

Time passes and I'm not sure how long we stand there, me holding her in her time of need, but when she straightens up and stands tall, you'd never know she's scared to death she'll go home a widow.

"Right now, he's just starting to come out of sedation. It's likely he'll need intense physical therapy, if not a wheelchair for life," she says. Looping her arm through mine, we begin the slow trek down the hallways to Dan's room. "They don't think he'll be paralyzed, but there's still a chance. His spine wasn't severed, but there's damage."

"How much?"

"Enough to not know until they test his nerves and reflexes." She swallows hard and I feel myself mimic the action. I can't imagine all the extra emotions she's feelings. Offering me a strengthening smile, she says, "They were waiting until our daughter arrived. Now that you're here, maybe they'll get things started."

I know for years they've considered me to be theirs, but hearing her say it in this moment is huge for me. There have been so many emotions in the last twenty-four hours. I can't say I'm overwhelmed by this, because how does one become more overwhelmed when they're already overwhelmed? It's a lot to absorb. All of it.

"I'm glad you consider me your daughter even after all these years," I say. I don't know why I say it, and it's out before I think to stop the words.

"Dan and I have always thought of you like that. The night you arrived, we decided that we were going to be your last home," she says. "It's bothered him for years that you didn't want to be adopted."

Pulling away from her, we stop in the middle of the hallway. I couldn't have heard her correctly.

"Why would you think I didn't want to be adopted?"

The creases at the corners of her eyes deepen and the skin above the bridge of her nose wrinkle.

"Because you told us. Sweetheart, it was one of the very first deep conversations we had. You came to me and asked if you could stay forever. I told you, 'Of course.' Your response was, and I'll never forget the way you looked at me when you said it because you were so filled with hurt, you said, 'Don't get any crazy ideas. No one actually wants to keep a teenager. I just need a bed to sleep in and you can act like I'm yours if that's what you want.',", she says quietly. "Lilah, you were so convinced no one wanted you, you refused to let us do anything about it even after your mother died. When you told us to just pretend, we did. We've been your legal guardians since you came to us, but adoption was brought up once after that, and it was never mentioned again. You have always been ours with or without the official paperwork and a name change. You don't remember that?"

"I was fifteen and angry, Mom," I say, feeling the tears begin to burn the backs of my eyes. "I don't remember that at all. No one wanted me. I was sure you and Dad wouldn't want me either."

She laughs and wipes away the tears that escape down my cheeks. All these years I've just accepted that I was unadoptable, destined to be a foster forever, and I told them no? Why would I tell them no?

"If you only knew. Dan saw you the night you came to us and decided out of all the kids we'd fostered over the years you were the one he wanted as our forever daughter. There you were in the kitchen baking away, red hair all pulled back in braids, and he just felt like you belonged with us. You brought us more joy in the first five days you lived with us than we had experienced in five years," she says. "And before you overthink it, I felt the pull to keep you the moment I opened the front door to welcome you home. We have never thought of you as anything but our daughter, Delilah. Never."

"But why wouldn't you push the topic? Eventually I wasn't angry anymore. We could have talked about it," I say.

She sighs deeply and smiles sadly. As she links her arm with mine again and pulls me back into stride with her, she says, "Eventually, yes, you weren't angry anymore. You had adjusted to life with us, but Dan and I decided we weren't going to take a chance that asking would make you want to leave. So, we just lived happily ever after with you and have told everyone ever since you moved that our daughter Delilah is living her dream as a pastry chef."

"Adopt me now, then." That's crazy. I'm an adult. Can I even be adopted now? What is the matter with me? "Not right now, but we can always make it official before I get too much older."

"Okay," she says, laughing. "And then I can also officially call Genevieve and Jaxson my grandbabies once that's finalized, too."

My home study has been completed and I was approved for adoption even before the kids' parents' rights were terminated. This process was in the works before I met them. My circle is so small, Evelyn is the only one who knows any of this other than Mom and Dad. Mom has told me I have a savior complex. I tell her I just want to be someone's forever family like they were for me. I guess, despite all the conversations over the last year or so, she didn't read between all the lines that said I wanted to be theirs for real.

"The only problem I'm going to run into now is the smaller apartment. Hopefully that can happen quickly, but I know the system doesn't always work efficiently which is my saving grace right now," I say as we stop beside a door. A medical chart labeled "LANDRY" hanging out in the file holder tells me we've arrived and I feel the air in my lungs get stuck.

Pushing the door open slowly, I see his legs covered by a thin hospital blanket first and the machines filling him with medication and taking vital signs after. Slowly, I approach the bed, Mom behind me offering silent support, though she's the one who should be supported. His cheeks are pinked and his breathing is normal, but it looks like the sedatives are still working.

I slip my fingers into his hand not expecting much. I'm not paying much attention when I hear his voice, gruff and groggy, say, "Lilah, you came home."

He squeezes my hand carefully, and it reminds me of the times he would sit and answer the difficult questions I would ask about life and love and the future. Dan always made it easy to smile regardless of how difficult a topic might be.

"Of course, I came home. It's not everyday your Dad gets shot. You do realize there are easier ways to get me to come visit, right?" I smile, and he smiles, too.

"I always do things the hard way."

"Yeah, you do, but I love you anyway."

Chapter 26

Fisher

"You, my favorite leader of the waitstaff, are going to figure it out. I need to talk to Delilah and find out how long she needs to be here and then I'll let you know." I lick my ice cream cone and wink at Jax. "Doris, I have faith in you. Plus, Jacelyn is nearby if you need someone to make a business decision before I get back."

She's nervous about me being out of town on such short notice, and I fully understand her apprehension. The last time I took off unexpectedly, I was gambling and a total mess. That's not my life anymore.

"I'll call after the dining room is closed tonight to check in and give you an update. Like I said, though, if there's anything you need —"

"I know, I know. Call Jacey. I got it," Doris says. "Take care of that nice girl of yours. We're all hoping her pop pulls through."

She always referred to my dad as "Pop," and the endearment gives me a chuckle. I tell her I will and thank her again for holding down the fort while I'm gone. When the call disconnects, Jax and Genevieve are both staring at me. They're studying me. I wonder if I measure up. What father figures have they had aside from Dan? Were they good to them? I have a thousand questions and no answers.

"You live in a house?" Jax asks out of the blue.

"I do."

"Lots of bedrooms?"

"Four of them."

"And you don't have anyone else living in that house with you?"

"Jaxson, stop." Genevieve sounds like a mother hen, but they've been on their own in a sense so her scolding and protectiveness don't surprise me. "That's not a thing you ask someone. Fisher, it sounds like you have a very nice home."

My mouth opens to say thank you, but I hear myself say instead, "You're so mature for your age. Have you been allowed to be a kid at all?"

The shrug tells me everything I need to know.

"Delilah has an apartment. She's said it's small and she's looking for a bigger one," she says.

I hear a tiny voice in the back of my brain and ignore it the best I can. It's telling me to help give these children a home. It's not my place. This is Delilah's.

"Oh? She hadn't mentioned she was apartment shopping," I say. After all, it is the truth because she hadn't said anything about that to me. It makes sense though. There's no way she can take in two kids with a one-bedroom apartment.

I bite the bottom off my ice cream cone and suck the rest of the dessert through the tiny hole before eating the waffle cone. The kids follow suit and do the same as we walk toward the park exit.

"Probably," Genevieve begins, "because she's been burned by enough people to have trouble opening up. I'm just guessing."

It sounds like way more than a guess, and I'm pretty sure she's got a better idea than I do how much Delilah has trouble trusting others. Being bounced around the system, an absent father, a mother who cares one minute and then disappears the next would do that to a person. It's not even trusting men she has an issue with. It's everyone. I've seen her open up to Evelyn and Maggie, but she's known them a lot longer than me and I accept that things take time. I'll love her through it.

I nod at Genevieve and smile weakly.

"I'd guess you're right," I say quietly as she and Jax sandwich me on the sidewalk.

"But, if she finds a bigger place soon, maybe it won't take so long to bring us home," Jax says, suddenly sounding much younger than he is.

I don't look down when I feel them each take one of my hands in theirs while we stroll along the bustling walkway.

I don't question how right their small fingers feel in my palms.

*****

Delilah: HE HAS FEELING IN HIS LEGS!

Me: That's amazing news! How is he feeling overall?

Delilah: He feels good considering. They're moving him to a regular medical floor tonight.

I release a deep breath and share the good news with the kids while we wait for our milkshakes. We found this little diner that's decked out like it's 1955 and Big Bopper is playing on the radio. When Jax and Genevieve start jumping and yelling joyfully, it makes a scene.

"What's going on?" our server asks me, a smile on her face.

"We just found out our foster dad is going to be okay!" Jaxson yells at her, a thousand-watt grin lighting up his face.

"Well, that is awesome, little man." She looks at me for some sort of clarification. I quickly and quietly explain what happened. Her face pales. "Oh my gosh, I know him. He and Julie come in all the time for their date days."

Our walk has taken us all over the neighborhood, but it's just like home. Someone always knows someone else. Big city, but small town.

"Let Julie know we're thinking of them, please. The milkshakes are on the house," she says, before turning from the table and heading back toward the counter.

The kids are itching to return to the hospital. We grab our shakes and as I slide out of the booth, slip my wallet from the pocket of my jeans. I tip the table the amount the shakes would have cost, plus a little extra. I notice Genevieve watching my actions, a perplexed look on her face but she doesn't say anything to me about it.

Jaxson is ahead of us as we walk back in the general direction of the hospital, and I expected Genevieve to walk with her brother. The two seem inseparable. She surprises me, though, as she stays in step with me behind him.

"Why did you do that? She said the shakes were free," she says, the straw set against her lip as she speaks.

My cup dangles from my fingers and I glance at her as I lift it to my mouth and take a sip.

"Because they weren't free," I say.

Her brows knit together. She thinks hard for a moment, but comes up empty.

"Did you know I own a restaurant?" She shakes her head. "I do. I've learned over the years, when a server tells somebody that something is on the house, either the restaurant eats the cost or the server pays for whatever it is."

"So ..." she begins, but stops. The confused look returns.

"I saw the waitress pull her tips from her apron and pay our bill. She probably worked really hard for that small amount of money, and I appreciate her caring enough about Julie and Dan to make sure she doesn't go without."

Genevieve smiles, sips her shake, and says, "If Delilah doesn't marry you, can we still hang out?"

We laugh together and I wrap my arm around her shoulder.

"You and Jax will always be welcome," I say.

Somehow these two children I just met are supposed to be part of my life, and it is the strangest feeling I have ever felt to care about people I don't know. I could say it's because Delilah cares about them, but it's deeper than that.

Delilah

I hate leaving all of them, but Fisher and I need to get back.

"Text me when you get home, okay?" Mom says.

"I will. I don't like having to go so soon. Are you sure you don't need me to stay?"

Dan's on the mend and should be released from the hospital in a few days. It's practically a miracle he wasn't paralyzed and will have outpatient physical therapy to help him regain his strength. As a family, though, we've decided Genevieve and Jaxson are the last children he and Julie will foster. If I'm able to find a larger apartment, maybe we can speed up the process of adopting, but we're dealing with a state agency. It's unlikely anything will move quickly.

"Go. We'll be fine and we'll talk every day."

She hugs me tightly one more time. Genevieve and Jax hug me. Then they hug Fisher. Then they pull me and Fisher and Julie into a group hug. We collectively take a deep breath in our huddle and then break apart so Fish and I can return to Brockport.

I wave as we pull away from the house, feeling strangely calm about the entire weekend. I sync my phone with the Bluetooth system in Fishers SUV and turn on some Ella Fitzgerald while he pulls into a drive-thru for coffee. Fisher side-eyes me.

"What?"

"Nothing."

"Lies. You don't care for my music choices?" I ask. It doesn't bother me if he doesn't. It's not normal music for someone my age to love. Sometimes it feels like most people in their just-barely-30s are still acting like horny teenagers on the weekend and going to clubs and bars. I've never been that person. I like old things — music, dresses, other people's traditions.

"It's just different," he says, pulling forward in line to get our drinks. "Thank you. Have a great day! Not bad different, Delilah. More like I can see you singing along to it and baking in my kitchen kind of different."

I smile at the image he creates in my head as we pull back out into traffic. His kitchen is such a haven for someone like me. I take every opportunity I can to help him make dinner when we're together there.

"I have four bedrooms," he says.

It comes out of nowhere. Or so that's the feeling at first. I stare at his profile, the relaxed jaw and three days of beard growth, the way his lips pout all on their own in a kissable way. It's the slightest hint of a smirk that clues me in.

"Genevieve."

"She mentioned you were looking for a bigger apartment," he says, glancing at me quickly.

I purposely let out a dramatic sigh. There are things I need to remember to not talk to the kids about until they're set in stone.

"I was going to tell you," I say, quietly, feeling ashamed I haven't talked to him about anything really. Nothing of much substance anyway. "I'm not used to having a support system, Fisher. This is so new it's scary."

He lifts his cup to his mouth and I watch him carefully blow into the small drink hole before tipping it enough to get a taste of the liquid. I don't understand how he can drink it so hot, but until recently I also couldn't understand why people like coffee. He's changing my mind about a lot of things.

"It is kind of scary," he admits. "But I like it. I more than like it, Delilah. I love that you are here putting yourself out there for these kids. I see why you care about them so much. They remind me of Tommy's nephew and niece. I met Britton when he was a little younger than Jax. That kid can make your worst day become the best without doing anything special. Your kids just vibrate with positivity and it doesn't matter where they've come from or what they've endured."

I laugh, not because it's funny but because he gets it.

"I see they crawled into your chest cavity and claimed you as theirs as well," I say.

"Maybe a little." He shrugs and is quiet. We're both lost a little in thought when I hear, "I think you should move into the house. I know it's really soon and we're still getting to know each other, but I feel it in my gut."

"Are you sure it's not the coffee?" I say to lighten the mood and he shoots me a look.

"It could be, but I've been feeling it since my walk about town with them yesterday, so that's some powerful coffee," he says, smiling at me.

"I'll think about it," I say, responding to his suggestion while trying to calm my racing heart.

*****

It's been hours of comfortable conversation. We've talked about work things and his family and a bit about my family. I've tried to build a pro-con list in my head about moving into his house. For instance, a pro is getting to spend time with him without constantly having to compare schedules. Con, we haven't done anything in the bedroom. Nothing. I mean, there's been plenty of kissing and a lot of under the shirt but over the bra kind of stuff, but that's as far as it's gone. I'm not sure how it makes me feel. On one hand, I'm honored to know he's not just looking to get laid. On the other ...

"Are you afraid to have sex with me?" I blurt out as we pull into his driveway.

Radio. Silence. Oh, fuck. He is. He is afraid to be more intimate and now I'm probably not going to bother moving in because it's going to be weird. Shit.

He pulls into the garage and kills the engine. The door comes down behind us and we're bathed in soft darkness. The air is so thick, my brain starts working overtime and I'm pretty sure if he doesn't say something soon more stupid things will come out of my mouth.

"I'm not afraid. In fact, I'd like to do that very much. Most of the time when you're around I have trouble focusing. All I want is to do things to your body that make every inch of your skin blush the way your cheeks do when I say something dirty," he says, his voice gravelly and hoarse.

My brain doesn't process the words, but my body feels every single syllable. Without thinking, my thighs rub against one another to alleviate the pressure, but It only builds more.

"Are you worried about moving in because we haven't —"

"Not at all," I cut him off. "But, if you're serious about me living in the same space as you, that might be something we want to, you know, take care of."

"Like a bank transaction?"

Between being ridiculously horny and him always finding a way to make light of things, I can't help but want more with him.

"Exactly. Just like a bank transaction. But with condoms and bodily fluids," I say.

"I think I can handle that," he says, then unbuckles my seatbelt.

His hand brushes my hip and I'm pretty certain I either need to take my clothes off as I'm walking through the house or they just won't be coming off at all before this happens.

"We need to hurry this up," I say with some urgency in my voice. "It's been a long five months."

He unbuckles his belt and then stops moving. Slowly, he turns his head toward me.

"Five? Months?" His lip lifts in a smirk. "We've only been seeing each other for six-ish weeks, though."

"Yeah, well, I was busy staring at your ass after you argued with your sister about potatoes and my vibrator got plenty of workouts from that image alone. Can we go now?" I feel my cheeks flare and open the door to climb out, his laughter howling behind me.

Fisher meets me at the back of the car and pulls me hard against him. Everything is hard. His biceps, his abs, his cock straining against the fabric of his jeans.

"I am madly in love with you Delilah O'Brien," he says, his fingers weaving their way through my hair as he pulls my forehead against his. "Madly."

"Me too. Now take me to your bed and show me."

Chapter 28

Fisher

Holy fuck.

We waited how long for this?

It was worth every morning of waking up hard and every evening saying goodnight without burying myself inside her. Today, which turned into tonight, was worth all of it.

Delilah's sound asleep, her head on the pillow and my arm slid beneath her neck as I cradle her body against mine, but I can't fall asleep. It's not that I'm not exhausted. I'm just too inside my own head, thinking about things like proposals and adoptions.

My phone buzzes on the nightstand beside me and as much as I don't want to pull myself away from her warmth, it's not the first time it has made noise since we crawled into bed.

Jacelyn: You home yet?

Jacelyn: Are you working tomorrow?

Jacelyn: How is Delilah? Is her Dad going to be okay?

Plus, about a hundred other messages from her and Tommy. I might be exaggerating, but it feels like there are that many unread texts.

Tommy: Coffee at the Bean in the morning. See you bright and early.

That's the most recent one, so I reply.

Me: Coffee. Got it. Let Jace know we're home, I'm working tomorrow, and Dan is going to be good to go with some physical therapy. I haven't read the rest of her messages and I'm not going to tonight. Goodnight.

I barely shift my arm to set the phone back on the nightstand and it buzzes again.

Tommy: Are you sick? Do you have a fever? It's only 9.

I smile. He'll understand.

Me: We've been making up for lost time. Goodnight, T.

Instead of saying anything, he sends a thread of gifs that are all mildly suggestive before finally giving up.

Delilah shifts next to me and I watch her breathing. Her chest lifts gently and relaxes with each exhalation, the pulse point in her neck throbs slowly, and I'm certain I want to fall asleep like this for the rest of my life. That scares the shit out of me, though, because I'm so used to being alone and I don't want to mess this up. A few years ago, I was the big brother worrying about his sister moving too quickly with her very new boyfriend. Now, here Delilah and I are moving from barely friends to falling in love in the span of a heartbeat. I didn't think it was possible. I didn't ever believe I would find someone whose pieces fit so well with mine.

There's a red tendril curling behind her ear and I lean in to place a soft kiss against her neck. The stubble on my chin scratches against her shoulder. Her back presses into me more solidly and it's heavenly.

I don't remember the last time I felt complete

.

Chapter 29

Delilah

It's been five months of absolute insanity.

Waking up in Fisher's bed is icing on the cake. If someone would have told me the first night I met him that this would be where I end up, I would have laughed them out of my kitchen. Insanity.

I reach my right arm out and feel for him beside me. The sheet is still warm, so he couldn't have gotten up long ago. Sliding out of the king size bed, I search for clothes to pull on over my still naked body.

Last night, Fisher grabbed clean clothes out of the dresser and set them in the attached bathroom, so I wander toward the tall bureau. The large top drawer is filled with boxers, T-shirts and socks. I help myself to a shirt and shorts and hope he doesn't mind.

Would he mind? The question stumps me temporarily. This is new territory for us. I have no idea if he's super possessive of his boxer shorts or is the type of man who truly doesn't care if his girlfriend borrows a pair. What if he sees me in his clothes and demands I wear my own? I grab my bag from the weekend and start dumping things out to find the emergency underwear I keep in a Ziploc in the bottom. I can just wear my clothes from yesterday again, but dirty underpants? No.

I'm crouched down on my side of his bed, on the opposite side of the door, when I hear him clear his throat.

"Whatcha doin' down there?"

Slowly I stand up, feeling guilt rush coldly down my spine. My face feels instantly flushed.

"I was looking for clean clothes," I say.

His eyes travel from mine, down my body, and back up.

"It looks like you found some," he says, his tongue darting out to wet his bottom lip. "Come, breakfast is ready."

He reaches his hand out. Dropping the plastic bag of backup panties in my backpack, I take his hand and let him lead me toward the doorway.

"You're not upset I'm wearing your clothes?"

"Um, no. Why would I be upset about that?" He shakes his head and I hear the humor in his voice.

"Well, I didn't ask, for starters. Second, I wasn't sure if you were against sharing clothes and borrowing some would violate the sanctity of our relationship. This could have gone really poorly and not at all in my favor," I say, shyly.

We're halfway down the stairs when he stops and turns to me. We're practically eye-to-eye with him a step or two below me and I fall in love with everything about him even more.

"I would be offended if you didn't make yourself at home here. You can wear my clothes any time you want to. But," he says, his eyes growing a little darker, "after last night, I want to be the only person to take them off you for the remainder of my days on this earth."

My eyes widen and my lips part slightly as I try to grasp all the words he said.

"How long are we talking?"

"Decades, hopefully."

"Did you just…"

He scrunches his nose and looks up toward the ceiling before answering me.

"I think that's what I did," he says, like it's no big deal.

"Then I think my answer is yes. For now. I need to finish deciding if I don't hate you anymore," I say.

He steps up onto the stair I'm standing on and places his lips against my forehead.

"You know you're always going to love telling people how much you hated me at first," he says, smiling at me. "And I'm going to love telling those same people how scared I was to let a fiery little redheaded fairy steal my heart while acting like I hated her."

"It was an act?" I cock an eyebrow and flash a small smile.

"Let's just say it was how my inability to deal with my emotions presented itself. I turn into an asshole when I can't control certain aspects of my life." He gently places his hands on either side of my face, cupping my jaw and pulling me toward him. "It's not a great quality to have and I'm sorry for all the bullshit those first several weeks."

Lifting my face to his, I touch his nose with the tip of mine. He places his forehead against mine and I feel. I feel everything. I feel his apprehension and his adoration. I feel my need to find a family and my joy at realizing I have one right here. I feel it all.

"In that case, then, absolutely yes."

*****

"You're what!?"

I pull the phone away from my ear as Maggie screeches into it. It's been two days since Fisher and I returned from Long Island. I went to work the next day and at the end of my shift officially put in my notice at the grocery store. Maggie wasn't working with me and today is a scheduled day off, so I'm at Evie's working on designs for a wedding cake order I took just before leaving last weekend.

"I'm done. I am going for it. I was going to anyway, but now it's for real. My last day is two weeks from yesterday," I say, and then I pause. "I don't want you to think you have to do the same thing. I'm not so overwhelmed I would need you full-time yet, so take the time you need to figure out how this works for you."

I hear background noise at the grocery store since she's at work and then it's super quiet, which tells me she's gone into the backroom to talk to me.

"I already told them I want to cut my hours," she says. "I'm going down to part time starting next week."

I raise a fist in the air and do a silent happy dance.

"That is fantastic. I cannot wait to see what we can do, Maggie. This is going to be amazing," I say. "I am going to need all the help I can get once I get into wedding planning mode."

Oh shit.

"Wedding what? For who? You're going to add event planning to the baking? You're going to kill yourself doing too much too soon."

I smack myself in the forehead with my palm. I haven't even told Mom about the staircase proposal.

"Well ... not exactly."

"Oh. My. Gosh."

She connects the dots.

"You? And Mr. Reilly? Married?"

"Just a little bit."

She begins laughing hysterically. I cannot keep myself from joining her with my own giggle fit.

"When did that happen?" she asks as she's catching her breath.

"The morning after we got back from my parents'. There isn't even a ring to show off. So much has happened. I'll be at Evie's late. Stop over when you get off work and I'll bring you up to speed," I say, trying to end the conversation. I know she needs to get back to work and I absolutely need to focus on these designs or they won't be done when I need them to be.

Maggie gives me an affirmative and we hang up. Popping my earbuds in and turning on some Bob Marley, I get to work.

*****

I haven't had a lot of time to myself lately and I wonder what it's going to be like when the adoption is final. Then it hits me. Dan and Julie said they would adopt me now as an adult, then I'm going to adopt the kids, and at some point Fisher and I are going to get married ... and that's a lot of names changing. Not to mention, does he want me and the kids or just me? Because I'm soon to be a package deal and I'm quickly realizing this super easy relationship I have could actually be really fucking complicated.

Doodling away on more wedding cake designs, my mind continues to wander.

I don't actually need Dan and Julie to formally adopt me for them to be my parents. They've been in that role almost my entire life. They're legally my guardians, or were until I became an adult, and that was always enough. They loved me anyway. Adopting me is something that would make us feel good. The truth is, I already feel amazing knowing they chose to keep me forever regardless of me apparently telling them I didn't want to go through the legal process.

I'm okay with this.

I make a plan to call Mom in the morning and talk to her about it. I want her input. More than anything, I don't want to hurt her and Dad by not going through with it.

As I color in the lace pattern I've drawn on my sketchpad, I decide I need to talk to Fisher about the kids. Tonight. I can't let this sit because if he says he's not interested in jumping right into a parenting role with me, we're done. I can't be with him if he doesn't accept me, Genevieve, and Jax as a complete set.

Adding some powder blue to the design, I feel the remnants of warm summer air as it sneaks into the kitchen when the door to the parking lot opens. I assume it's Maggie, until I see his hand set a take away cup down in front of me. Then he adds a salad and a dish with lasagna.

I pull an earbud out and look at him.

"You haven't answered any of my messages, so I figured you were working intently. I brought fuel for you."

Without a word, I stand up on my tip toes and kiss him like it could be the last kiss I share with him. Because it could be the last one. I can't lie to myself. He could walk away from all of this right now.

"Is everything okay?" he questions, worry marring his face, as we break away from one another.

"Do you want to be their dad? Like, adopt them with me? Or are you going to—"

"Yes," he says. "That's what I was hoping. If that's what you want. We haven't really talked about that part of this."

I look at him closely, wondering if he'll flinch, but he doesn't move a muscle.

"We haven't really talked about any of this. Nothing. I don't know how to do this."

"Do what?"

"Love you and the kids and be in a relationship and plan a wedding and start a business and ... all of it. How do I balance it all?"

Fisher reaches out and firmly grasps my shoulders. He pulls the corner of his bottom lip between his teeth and bites. Is he afraid of hurting me? Is he contemplating what we're actually talking about doing here? Is he already regretting us?

"Balance is tricky."

I try really hard to not roll my eyes and he can see it. His fingers trail along my shoulders until he laces them at the back of my neck, placing his thumbs on my jaw so we're looking each other in the eyes.

"Balance is asking for help when you need it instead of waiting until you are so overwhelmed you cry from the stress. Balance is choosing to be here today working to get it all done instead of coming to the restaurant for dinner with me. Balance is going to be scheduling appointments for the kids and moving appointments you've made for yourself. And it's going to be making sure we take time for just us sometimes, because relationships are work no matter how good two people are together."

"But what if I can't manage it? I've only had me to worry about. You're already the longest relationship I've ever had, but we haven't had to do life together because it's still been such a short amount of time," I say, my hands waving furiously with the words.

"You aren't going to be doing any of this alone," he says, his lips against my forehead.

"How can you say that? You're at the restaurant twelve hours a day. I'm here or at the store all the time and now that I'm done working at the store in a couple weeks, I'll be here even more. We are literally not together all the time."

"Not physically, but that doesn't mean jack shit and you know it," he says. Point blank honesty is probably his last resort. "What do you mean you're done at the store?"

I pull back a little so I can see his face.

"Business has been good and I can do more if I'm not splitting my time. I already make more hourly doing this than I do at my real job."

A tiny part of me is extremely proud of how far I've come. I've stopped letting the fear of moving forward hold me so tightly I can't breathe. Dad being in the hospital has really driven home the fact this life isn't guaranteed.

However, another tiny part of me is so damn scared I'm going to screw all of this up and end up homeless and jobless.

Then he smiles a smile that makes the worry melt away. His fingers leave my face. Before I'm aware of what he's doing with his hands, I'm lifted into the air, wrapped into the tightest hug I've ever had.

"I am so proud of you, Delilah." Fisher's voice is the quiet approval I didn't think I needed, but wanted nonetheless. "It's all coming together."

"Do not jinx it."

"It's coming together with hard work and a lot of maneuvering and love?"

"Better."

Chapter 30

Fisher

It's been a long time since all the bedrooms in my house have been used. I think the last time they all had beds in them was when Jacey was still in college in California. After our parents died and Jacelyn wasn't coming home for more than a few days at Christmas, I took down the ones that weren't needed. That left my parents' bedroom set. Over the years, I've switched out the mattress, but everything else in their bedroom has remained the same.

"Do you want your bedroom set? The one you had when you were a kid?" I ask my sister. I make it sound like a normal, run-of-the-mill question that any homeowner would ask.

She lifts an eyebrow at me and turns to place her hand on the bar.

"I don't think so. You are welcome to do what you want with it," she says. "Is there something you want to do with it?"

It's been a month since I proposed to Delilah and we decided to adopt Genevieve and Jaxson together. As a unit. She's my puzzle piece, and the kids complete the picture. The thing is, we haven't told anyone, with the exception of Maggie, Julie, and Dan. It's not that we don't want to tell people — just the opposite, in fact. We want to share our news once we have things squared away for the kids, though. We're in the process of getting them moved to Brockport so we can foster to adopt since there's no chance of reunification. We haven't talked with anyone about it outside of Delilah's parents, though.

I've been doing a lot of reading and studying on all of this, and I love Delilah more for how much she went through as a kid. I love her even more knowing she wants to provide a safety net for others. Gen and Jax likely won't be the last children we foster, though they are the last ones for Dan and Julie.

"Nothing in particular," I say to Jacey.

When she crosses her arms and gives me a "mmm hmm," my fight or flight kicks in and I start toward the kitchen.

"Fisher?"

"Yeah?" I respond without turning around.

"Is she pregnant?"

Stopping halfway across the room I act like I'm pushing in a chair and fixing a table arrangement. I know my sister well enough to know she won't take a simple "no" as an answer, even though it's the truth.

"She is not pregnant. That's not even something we've talked about," I say. Looking at Jacelyn I see her face fall a little as she touches the bump that's forming beneath her shirt. That alone tells me she was hopeful there was another cousin on the way.

"Oh. Okay," she says. "Then, why the bedroom set?"

"Because someday the bedrooms in the house we grew up in are going to have little people living in them again. Just not right this second," I say. It's not a big lie, right? There she goes giving me emotional eyes again and I feel my heart squeeze in my chest because this is my baby sister. I can't lie to her at all. "Maybe in a couple months though."

Her mouth drops open with a question, but I can see she isn't sure what question it is she should be asking.

"But you just said ... How in a couple months if she's not pregnant? What are you up to?" she says, placing her hands on her hips.

If I don't tell her, she's going to text Delilah. I don't want drama, and my sister doesn't do drama, so this just needs to be dealt with.

"We're in the process of bringing Genevieve and Jaxson here. We're planning to adopt, but fostering first. It's a whole thing," I say. Her eyes go wide. "Yeah."

"Is that allowed since you aren't married?"

"Well ..."

"You got married without telling me?" Her screeching is ear-piercing and I slam my hands against my head to block the sound.

I did not see that response coming. We've definitely talked about eloping and getting it done and over with, but I wouldn't do that without Jacelyn and Tommy knowing first. I see her waiting for my response and I sort of want to wait it out just to be mean, but she's pregnant and super emotional this time.

"No," I say, and she throws her hands up in frustration.

"You're fucking infuriating, Fisher."

Laughing I say, "I know, right? Think how Delilah feels having to live with me. How about this? You and T come for brunch Saturday. We'll bring you up to speed."

Rolling her eyes as I walk over to her, she says, "Fine. What do you want me to bring?"

I pull my little sister into a hug and squeeze her tightly, thankful she's going to let it go for tonight.

"Just you and T and my little shadow."

She nods and hugs me back, then squeezes tighter as she lets her breath out against my shoulder. "If Genevieve doesn't want my bed set, I'll help you buy a new one."

"I love you, Jacey. Mom and Dad would be really proud of us."

"Yeah, I know. They raised some damn good kids."

*****

Saturday rolls around and I'm up before the sun getting food ready. Delilah and I decided to turn the morning into a whole meet and greet event. Informal invitations were sent to my sister and Tommy, Brian and Stella, Steph and Max, Caryn and Greg, Mama and Ben, Jenny and Dale, Maggie, and Evie. I left Doris off the list because she goes to Saturday Mass and I didn't want to give her one more reason to pray for me.

Delilah has met everyone over the course of her time working at the grocery store and then when she and I started seeing one another, she became further acquainted. I think she hears from Tommy's mama more than I do these days.

"Good morning," she says as she passes behind me to get to the refrigerator. "I had the weirdest dream last night. There was this woman standing at the end of our bed and she just kept saying, 'You're doing great, kiddo.' No idea who she was."

I tlp my head slightly as I whip the eggs for the quiche.

"It was so real. I would have sworn I was awake, but I don't think I was. That would have been even more strange, right?" she says. "She looked a lot like Jacelyn, too."

She lifts a glass of orange juice to her lips and I stop to stare at her.

"Have you seen a picture of my mom and dad?"

Her dream feels really real to me. I've had the same one.

For years.

"I … thought I had. It's not like there aren't pictures in the house, but I don't think I've paid too close attention."

She gets a confused look on her face. I hold my hand up in an effort to get her to stop thinking about it for just a moment.

"You don't think I had a dream about your mom, do you?"

She begins to laugh and it slowly dies to a chuckle until she's staring at me waiting for a response.

"I'm just saying stranger things have happened around here," I say, grabbing my wallet from the kitchen drawer I keep it in at night. I know what my mom looks like in my dreams, so I pull a picture from my wallet and hand it to Delilah. "Yes?"

"Holy shit."

Yeah. Holy shit.

She touches the photo with the tip of her finger.

"You have her eyes. Jacelyn has her nose," she says, studying the picture. "She's beautiful. Why would she show up in my dream, though? I never got to meet her."

That's a great question, but I don't tell her that. Instead, I shrug, set the wallet on the counter, and continue whipping my eggs.

"It's comforting, whatever the reason. I haven't had a mom tell me I'm doing great, other than Julie, in a long time," she says, softly. "It's kind of nice to know my future mother-in-law thinks I'm doing okay right now, even if it was just a dream."

Delilah steps up next to me and slides the photo of Mom back into my wallet. I've stayed quiet, hoping she'll keep talking. I know she has things to say and I don't want to interrupt her thoughts or interject with my own theories.

"I'm not feeling as alone anymore, you know? You were right. I have family here. Sometimes it's just difficult to focus on the fact I have a support system," she says. "For a majority of my life it's felt like it's just been me, and it isn't easy to break the habit of not relying on other people."

"When even the dead are showing up in your dreams to offer you support, I think you're doing just fine, sweetheart," I say.

Setting the bowl down on the counter, I wipe my hands on the towel hanging from the waist of my sweatpants before pulling her against me. Her body relaxes into me.

"I love you."

Breathing in the scent of her shampoo, I realize I've forgotten what life was like before her. It was actually kind of boring. No wonder my sister and Tommy started getting after me to find a girlfriend.

"I love you, too. I'm glad I set my cupcakes up where your meat was supposed to be," she says. I feel her smile against my chest. "Not a euphemism."

"But," I say, looking at the clock on the wall, "we could potentially have time to make it one if we hurry."

I waggle my eyebrows at her seductively, which is more for humor than to get her into bed, and she places her index finger against her cheek like she's thinking about it.

"How much time are we talking?"

Chapter 31

Delilah

"... and that's how we got to this point," I say.

Fisher picks up his coffee, takes a sip, and lifts an eyebrow in my direction. I'm not sure if he's giving me a mental high five or if the look is because I should add more. I'll add more.

"It's a lot. We know it's a lot all at once," I say. "I would be lying if I said I don't panic inside every time I think about us adopting two kids who haven't ever been outside of New York City or seen a cow in person."

I can't read any of their reactions and it's a little intimidating. Maybe this was a bad idea, and as strong as I am I'm afraid to untwist my hands because they're going to shake uncontrollably. The only thing truly keeping me from standing up and fleeing is Evie, because she's known this was my plan from the beginning. Since I met them, I've wanted to bring them home. I want to be their last home, and now Fisher wants to be their last home, too, and it's more than I could have ever hoped for.

Mama Stratford is the first to do anything — move, breathe heavily, sigh — and she kind of does all three of those at once.

"Delilah," she says, in her sweet southern accent that I love so much, "you're talking to a group of people who love children. Raising babies is kind of what we do. What do you need from us? Beds? Clothes? School supplies? Make us a wish list."

Fisher and I look at one another. I'm sure my face conveys shock, but his is a big, fat, "I told you so."

"I hadn't thought in depth about any of those things yet. Beds, yes, a little because they need them. Clothes, they have what they need right now but they're children and grow quickly," I say. My voice is going to betray me but fuck it. "Really, I just wanted to be sure you will accept them as ours. Not as 'the kids Fisher and Delilah adopted,' but as our children. Just like you've accepted me."

Mama smiles at me, elbows Ben, and takes a drink from her mug. I try to get my emotions under control, but it's kind of pointless. I gather a few napkins in my hands.

"Okay, so, here's what we're going to do," she says to me. She's not talking to anyone else, just me. "You're going to get me a list of sizes for my new grandbabies, then Jenny and I are going to go shopping, and when we're done, those two will be set until at least Christmas. Deal?"

And here come the tears ...

"Now wait just a damn minute!" Steph slams her hands down on the table and pushes her chair back.

There's a lot of commotion as I watch Stella, Jacelyn, and Caryn stand up as well. There's a flurry of hands and heated whispering.

"We," Stella says, acting like the calmer of the sisters, "aren't going to be outdone by Mom and Mama. So, if they're buying all the clothes, we're in charge of decorating bedrooms and starting a snack cupboard. Kids love snacks. You just need to get us a list of favorites. Colors, movies, characters, foods, whatever."

I bury my face in my hands as I begin sobbing, mostly with relief that they are so accepting but also because I am so overwhelmed. I've never had family. Not like this. It didn't exist. Now, it's crawling out of the woodwork and showing up in my dreams.

"That's not fair. The ladies are picking all the fun stuff to take care of. What about me and Ben? What do we get to do?" Dale says above the quiet chatter created by the matriarchs.

I look up briefly and see Tommy, Brian, Max, and Greg contemplating something. They look from one to the other before Tommy wraps his arm around Brian and smiles at Stella's dad.

"Swing set!" they yell in unison.

Jacelyn scoots over and pulls us against her, Tommy gathers us all, and then the rest of them pile on, one at a time, hugging us all together. I feel all the love this family — my family — has to offer. I'm sure it always vibrates throughout the room when they're all together, but this morning it's them literally wrapping their arms around me and Fisher and lifting us up in support.

"I told you everything would work out," Fisher whispers in my ear. "Everything is gonna be alright."

"Can we also help plan the wedding?" Jacey whispers.

"I think I know a caterer," Tommy whispers.

"Why are we whispering?" Ben asks.

"Oh my gosh, I love you all so much," I say, unable to hold back my laughter as it mixes with my tears. "Is this how a normal family operates? I've only been in dysfunctional ones."

The pile of huggers begins to disperse, one at a time, and Fisher and I are able to sit up for air. He touches my cheek and winks at me.

"I think normal is a relative term. Some would think we're the dysfunctional ones. We say, 'I love you,' every time we hang up the phone and hug about ninety-seven times before leaving any event … and for us, that is normal," he says. "I hope that's okay with you."

Leaning in close, I press my lips against his for a quick kiss and pull away.

"If it wasn't okay, I wouldn't have stuck around to get to this point."

*****

Brunch turned into grazing all afternoon and visiting. Wedding planning has officially started. It's essentially finished as well. When you have a cake business, a friend with an awesome reception location, are marrying a man who owns a restaurant and caters events … well, it takes a lot of the hard decisions out of the equation.

"Three tiers and cupcakes?" Maggie asks.

"There aren't going to be enough people for three tiers." I'm not upset about that; I'm being logical. Neither of us are in a situation where there's a ton of extended family. With the exception of Dan, Julie, and the kids, pretty much our entire guest list is at the house right now. "We'll definitely do up plenty of cupcakes, though. We can send some home with everyone."

Maggie says she'll draw up design concepts for the cake. She doesn't want me making any of it, and I've decided giving her control of the cake is exactly what I need to do.

There are a lot of other events being planned that are keeping me busy with orders coming in, plus the phone calls every week asking about stopping into "the bakery" to pick up a few sweets. People are understanding when I tell them it's not a full-service bakery where people can just walk in off the street to grab a treat, but that doesn't stop them from wanting to come to Evie's farm and check the cooler for a snack. If I keep getting requests like this, I'm going to have to ask Evie about the possibility of a small cooler display case, but that's a conversation for another day.

Mags gives me a quick hug, breaking me from my thoughts, and tells me she's heading out.

"I need a shower and to get my hair all done up. I've got a hot date," she says, her cheeks turning a shade of pink I haven't seen before.

I give her a look that clearly says, "I need more information than that."

"He's an adjunct at the college. A musician named Alexander and he's kind of dreamy in a dorky way," she adds.

I offer her a "mmm hmm" and say, "Go get prettied up. I'll see you tomorrow."

Maggie claps her hands together energetically and I notice the bounce in her step as she picks her bag up off a chair. Joy looks good on her.

I'm alone for the first time since I woke up this morning and I take advantage of the moment. Doodling on a piece of scrap paper, I make a list of the things I'm grateful for right now.

The kids
Fisher
The whole family
My job
My bakery
The sunshine
Good music
Fancy dresses
A full life

Six months ago, I made a list like this. It had "my job" and "Julie and Dan" on it. So much can change in such a short amount of time. I don't think that's something a lot of us realize or stop to think about. I didn't until just now. I'm a different person than I was when I first started this journey. I've shed the skin that held me back from chasing dreams. Maybe I did something right in my last life to deserve all of this … maybe I just deserve it after years of working quietly in the background.

Chapter 32

DECEMBER
Fisher

We agreed on a Christmas wedding.

Why would we do that to ourselves?

Life for both of us is crazy at the holidays. Even before Delilah owned the bakery, she was so busy her life outside of work essentially stopped, but since the week before Thanksgiving she's been home to sleep and that's about it. Murph suggested we get the legal part of getting married out of the way so we can enjoy the rest of it, but that seems even more rushed.

I'm looking forward to taking her away for a bit before things get even crazier, though. Just for the rest of the weekend. The kids will be here with Dan and Julie for the wedding, then they're going to stay since they'll be on break from school for the holiday and our placement will be complete. By spring, we'll be parents and they'll be well settled into a new school with new routines. It's been a really long handful of months traveling between Brockport and Long Island to see them whenever we can, but worth every last drop of gasoline.

"How's the food coming?" Jacelyn says from the doorway.

I've been in here prepping pans of lasagna since five this morning, but I've been on autopilot and don't even know what time it is now.

"It's being made. Are we stupid for doing this?"

"For making lasagna for tonight's special? No. Everyone loves your lasagna." She stares at me, confused. She crosses her arms and uses her pregnant belly as a shelf to set them on. "Tell me what's up."

But, how? I breathe in deeply and place another layer of noodles in the pan in front of me.

"Rushing a wedding, rushing to adopt the kids, rushing everything," I say, shrugging as I do because if I don't, if I look up at her, I might cry. "This is a lot in a little amount of time. It's only been four months since we got engaged. What if I'm not cut out for it? What if I'm not the husband she needs or the dad they need?"

"The fact you're so worried, I think, shows you are cut out for it. You're an amazing man, Fisher, and I'm not just saying that because you're my big brother," she says. "Delilah's strong enough to have started the adoption process without a man in her life, but she wouldn't have said yes to you if she wasn't ready to share the load. She wouldn't have said yes to you if you weren't the right one for the job."

She isn't wrong. Delilah isn't the type to let someone in if she doesn't want to. I've seen her with people at the restaurant over the last few months when she has the chance to stop in, especially when she's waiting for me at the bar. Some asshole always tries to talk to her, and she shuts them down before they start. I like to think it's because she loves me that much, but a big part of it is the city in her. That sweet but tough girl attitude that I fell hard for.

"Do you think I'll be good enough for all of them?"

"What I think doesn't matter, but since you asked, yes. I think you're going to be so fucking good for them they won't know what to do with you. I think you're going to be a parent like our parents were and that says a lot because even I struggle to be like them a lot of days," she says.

That's the one thing I've wanted for a long time — to be like my dad. There were a lot of years I hated the idea of being like him. He worked constantly and always put other people before himself, and it made me angry when I was a young teen how everyone else was so much more important than him and, sometimes, us. But that was the lesson. Even with working all the time he was selfless. If we needed him, he was there. If someone at the restaurant needed him, he put them ahead of himself. He genuinely loved everyone and I hate that he's not here to see that I turned out okay-ish. I wish he was here to give me advice instead of my sister, regardless of how good her advice always is.

I finish putting together the pan of lasagna I've been working on and cover it with plastic wrap. I haven't responded yet and instead of opening my mouth to say anything, I start on the next pan. I'm not even sure what to say since I've been so deep in my own thoughts.

"Stop," she says.

"I can't," I reply.

"You're just like him," she says.

"In what way?" I ask.

"All of them. You always put us first. You come last. You have kept this place running no matter what—" I snort out a laugh, but she catches me off guard. "—even with a shitty gambling habit that could have lost it all."

My head snaps up and I stare at her. Wide-eyed and in shock, I can't even muster words.

"You thought I didn't know?" she asks, arms still crossed. She hasn't moved from her spot and I can't get over how much like Mom she is.

"I was pretty sure you didn't."

"Just because I was still across the country when it happened doesn't mean I wasn't going to find out," she says. "You talk a lot when you drink too much."

It's been a long time since I drank enough to not remember a conversation. That means she's known about the gambling and been keeping this from me for literal years.

"I didn't want you to be disappointed in me. I was afraid if you knew you would come home and try to fix it for me when it was something I needed to fix on my own," I say. "But I don't think it would have happened as smoothly as it did if it weren't for Tommy. I owe him a lot of gratitude for saving my ass."

Closing my eyes, I try to figure out how to apologize for being such a rotten person.

"Tommy is good at what he does, but all he did was guide you." She pushes off the doorframe and walks to the counter in the middle of the kitchen where I'm lining up the filled pans just so I have something to keep my hands occupied. "I would never be disappointed in you, Fish. I know it was hard. You quit school to keep this place afloat because it was Dad's dream, the family's dream. You made sure I stayed in school instead of booking it back home right after they died. You immediately jumped into that patriarch role and I am forever indebted to you for allowing me to keep being a college kid while you ran the family business. And the gambling? It's in the past. You've worked really hard to leave it there. I don't know all the details and I don't need to, so I don't want you to start explaining it all. Just keep me in the loop if you start feeling like you need to scratch that itch."

There aren't any words I can offer my sister. She responded to all the things I could have said without me saying a damn thing. So, instead, I open my arms and wait for her to walk around the counter to hug me. And we cry together because life hasn't been the nicest to us, but at least we've had each other.

Chapter 33

Delilah

Why did we decide on December? Why Christmas?

Because we both love the holiday and want to spend it with the kids. That's why.

I turn the cake I'm working on and pipe more buttercream around the base, slowly lifting my arm to create the perfect swirl up the side. Setting the scraper against it to smooth the frosting out I really start questioning why we aren't just going to the courthouse to get married. We can always just have a party after and call it done.

"Whatcha thinkin' 'bout?" Evie asks from the door.

"Weddings."

She laughs, but it doesn't sound like she finds humor in my response.

"You're always thinking about weddings. Whose wedding are you thinking about today, yours or the one you're making that cake for?"

I finish turning the cake and scrape the excess frosting back into the mixing bowl. Taking a deep breath, I say, "Maybe Fisher and I should just go to the courthouse. We have the marriage license, so it's just a matter of witnesses and saying the vows."

"If that's what you want, you should tell him."

"But I also want the walk down the aisle experience and have Father Murphy do his thing," I say. "I don't know what I want. We're only a couple weeks away from the wedding. It would be pointless to do it the other way now."

Evie nods, but doesn't offer any motherly advice.

"I just feel so stressed with everything else going on. How am I supposed to get married in the middle of all this? It doesn't even slow down that much after Christmas, and that's when the kids are going to officially be here."

Lifting up my planner filled with orders and due dates, I turn it so she can see. I'm swamped. More than swamped. I'm fucking drowning.

"If you give me a recipe I can help. Call Maggie and have her come in earlier," Evie says, stepping away from the door and heading toward the sink to wash her hands. "Asking for help is not a sign of weakness no matter what you've been telling yourself for God only knows how long."

I give her a look that clearly says, "Are you sure?" and hand over my cupcake batter recipe.

"We need a lot of cupcakes. Like, a lot," I say, feeling my emotions rise to the surface.

"Call, Maggie. I'll get started," she says, pulling me into a quick hug.

It doesn't take long for me to get back into my groove while we wait for Mags to get to the farmhouse. She stopped at the Jumping Bean and surprised me and Evelyn with giant cups of café mocha.

"I figured we're going to be here a while, so better get caffeinated," she says setting a cup down next to the sink behind me.

My kitchen rules are pretty strict these days — when I'm working, no extra foods or beverages in the workspace. I've had more than my fair share of close calls with spilled drinks near cupcakes and cookies. The last thing I want to have happen is someone's wedding treats be destroyed by my own carelessness.

"What are we working on?" she asks, as she dries her hands on a clean kitchen towel.

I hand her an apron and shrug.

"Everything," I say, pushing the planner in her direction as she ties the apron around her waist.

"This is nothing. We've done more with less before. No stressing," she says.

"She's also questioning the church wedding and how to make life with the kids work," Evie pipes in.

I turn and look at her, but as upset as I'd like to be that she shared that information, I can't be mad. These women have become some of my closest confidants and their support is what keeps me going. It's a lot different from where I was at the beginning of my story in Brockport when there was no one else pushing me.

Maggie sidles up next to me, a cooled cupcake in her hand, and offers a genuine "it's okay" smile.

"Everything is going to work itself out. You know this. Have faith," she says before quietly going to work.

*****

Four hours later we're working side-by-side comfortably, singing along with the Christmas music Evie turned on when she popped the first pan of cupcakes in the oven. There hasn't been conversation for a while and it makes me jump when Maggie starts talking like we were in the middle of one.

"Maybe going to the courthouse isn't such a bad idea. You just get it out of the way, then whatever happens the day of the big wedding just ... happens," she says, head bowed as she pipes frosting on a cooled cupcake. "It takes the stress off you and Fisher. Murph still gets to do the Christmas wedding. Dan gets to walk you very slowly down the aisle, which is a huge fucking deal since a few months ago walking at all was kind of iffy. Then, you can enjoy the day, get those first family photos of you guys and the kids, dance your ass off and get sweaty and gross without a care in the world."

I nod my head, but don't say anything. There are bigger things going on in my brain than just wedding things. I'm in the process of looking at a storefront. It's not something I thought I would do, but the small cooler case in Evie's kitchen isn't cutting it. There's someone in here every day buying treats, usually placing orders for dozens of treats or asking for custom cakes and cupcakes for birthdays and anniversaries. It's been difficult to keep up with the volume of orders, to say nothing about having extras on hand. Getting through the holiday and back into normal life will be the test. If business is still that steady, it's time to grow into a new space.

My plans never included staying at the farm forever. I don't think I knew what my plans really were until they were happening.

Maggie and Evelyn are busy chit-chatting while I'm lost in my thoughts. The cake I was working on when the day began is done for the time being and resting in the cooler. The massive amount of cupcakes that have been baked are mostly frosted. Another cake is almost ready to come out of the oven.

"I think I need to hire another person to help us out," I say, without a second thought.

Their chatter quiets.

"This has grown so much in such a short amount of time and I'm starting to wonder if an extra set of hands, even just part-time, would be beneficial," I explain, not quite sure of myself.

I'm always questioning myself. I hear the question in my voice, as though I'm asking for their permission to make a decision with this business. I haven't even mentioned window shopping for a store, but they aren't stupid. If I'm talking about another employee, they know I'm thinking about how we're running out of room here.

"You have grown. This hasn't, Lilah. It's all you," Evie says to me. "When you first started this, you were shoving cupcakes in the corners of your apartment just to make due. You could hardly ask for help even when I offered it. Look at you now. You shed that scared child skin and put on your fancy big girl dress and turned it all on its head."

Looking from one to the other of them, I give myself five seconds to decide.

"I'm going to put out feelers tonight and see if there's anyone local who can manage joining this crazy team. If I don't find anyone, I'll give a call to my advisor from college and see if she knows of anyone in need of some more hands on experience," I say. Guilt is starting to creep in that I haven't talked to Maggie about opening an actual store. What's it going to hurt? "I'm also in the market for an actual shop. I've been looking at some real estate and, once we get through the holidays, if things are still crazy, I'm taking the leap."

Maggie laughs. It's a full belly laugh and I wait for her to catch her breath.

"You're just leaping all over the place. Marriage and kids, looking for more help, setting up a real bakery," she says, her smile so big I'm afraid her cheeks are going to hurt. "Never in all the time we were at the grocery store did I think this is where you'd be right now. I am so stinking proud of you."

I'm proud of me, too, and that's a feeling I forgot how to have. I haven't slowed down long enough to even think about it.

Chapter 34

Fisher

When I walk in the house, I'm a little taken by surprise. Delilah has the kitchen torn apart and I can tell I've interrupted a major reorganizing event.

"Delilah?" I ask, clearly concerned. We've lived together long enough now to have started figuring out all the ins and outs of what makes each of us tick, but this is new.

"Yeah?" she calls out from inside a cupboard.

"What's up, sweetheart? Did you need help finding something?"

That's a dumb question. This woman knows every inch of space inside this room. It's like her haven. It's mine as well, but not like it's hers. Regardless, there's no way she can't find something.

"Just destressing. It was a productive day at Evelyn's and some of the conversation left me feeling overwhelmed about already being overwhelmed. So, now I'm just fixing the overwhelmed," she says, pulling more baking supplies from the cupboard. "It's totally normal to want to just get married before getting married to take the pressure off, right? That's a normal thing, yes?"

I can't keep myself from smiling. Here I've been panicking about rushing into marriage, and she's ready to take the plunge to be married sooner.

"Probably not normal, but unlikely it's not something a lot of people think about." I set my backpack down on an empty barstool and lean into the counter. "Is that something you want to do?"

She pops out of the cupboard and looks at me, an eyebrow raised in question.

"Do you?"

"We've got two weeks before the real wedding. If it'll make it easier on us to not stress about how the day is going to go, why wouldn't we just do it now?"

"Because people are going to think we're stupid for not just waiting. Except for Evie and Maggie. They both told me we should just do it so we can focus on having fun at the real wedding," she says.

While she's talking — louder now because she's stuffed herself back into the cupboard — I pull my phone out and start a new message.

Me: Are you allowed to marry us early as long as we have the license?

His response comes in under a minute.

Murph: I do what I want. Are we doing this now or do you two need time to talk?

Me: You do what you want within reason, Father. I know you well enough to know you are far from a rule breaker. Let me talk to her. I'll get back to you.

I set my phone on the counter and lean in again.

"Lilah?"

That gets her attention. It's like I yelled her name. I never call her Lilah and when I do it always rocks her a little. If I'm being honest, it does the same to me.

She backs out of the cupboard, a Twizzler hanging out of her mouth and a stack of odd baking supplies in her arms.

"Uh huh?"

Her eyes are wide and her face is drained of color.

"Do you have plans later this evening?" I ask.

We're both home exceptionally early, so I'm struck with a feeling of now or never. She turns back to the cupboard and then frees an arm, motioning to the messes on every usable surface.

"I will probably be up until midnight or later trying to organize all this. We need to go through expiration dates and use by dates and I'm thinking we'll put things back in order by size and shape. All the boxed things together, the cans of stuff in one spot. You know. Organized. Like adults who have their lives together," she says, finishing the sentence off with a bite of Twizzler.

"What about if I help you after we go visit Murph," I say. It's not a question like it should be, but that's because I can see her stressing out more as we stand in the kitchen staring at one another.

"You want to go visit Father Murphy tonight?"

Her eyebrows knit together and I see her watching me closely as I walk over to the binder she's put all the wedding info into. Slowly, I slide the envelope from the town clerk's office out of its pocket and hold it in front of me like an offering.

"Are you sure?" she asks, quickly emptying her arms.

Pulling another piece of red licorice from the bag, she steps toward me. I'll never tire of how tiny she is compared to me and I tip my head down to kiss her as she lifts up on her toes, meeting me halfway.

"Does heaven smell like a cupcake factory?" I ask pulling away just enough to get the words out.

"God, I love you," she says, mashing her lips against mine again. When she releases my mouth, she smiles and says, "Let's go get married."

Chapter 35

Delilah

"And that's pretty much the whole story," I say.

"Well, not the whole story," Fisher says, winking at me as he sets the mug of hot chocolate in front of me.

The Jumping Bean is the busiest I've seen it in a long time, but tonight is Greg's monthly open mic night. This is the first we've told anyone we're already married, with the exception of Jacey and Tommy. They were our witnesses, but they're also our best people and standing with us at the big wedding. Considering Jacelyn is Fisher's only sibling and I have none, it wouldn't have sat right with either of us if she wasn't there.

"So now you're calm and relaxed and ready for the big day?" Stella asks.

Fisher and I exchange a look before he responds.

"Yes, I think we are. All the major things were finalized before we went to see Murph, so now it's just party favors and making sure the ring bearer doesn't lose the rings. Right, T?"

Tommy puts his hand over his heart and gives a scout's honor.

"I promise I will not lose the rings."

I smile at him, knowing he would never jeopardize our wedding. Jacelyn would have a heart attack if he did.

The conversation is slow and easy, the atmosphere welcoming us into the fold as a couple. I think that's something I was unsure about — how will we fit in with all the couples? There are so many of us and everyone is tightly woven together. Joining the group was intimidating at best. But here we are on an evening when we would normally have a thousand things going on. It's our last free night before the kids arrive in town tomorrow and we have to really make solid plans instead of just running out the door last minute to go to dinner.

"Hey, Delilah," Jacey says, sliding into the seat beside me. I hadn't even noticed Fisher get up to go get something else from the café. "You look like you have worries. Wanna talk about it?"

A local college girl stands up by the window, an A Cappella version of a song I don't recognize coming out of her, the beat slow and volume low making it a little easier to hear when others are talking.

Shrugging my shoulders, I take a sip of my cocoa and try to hold in all the emotions I'm feeling.

"You know, when Fish and I were kids we used to talk about what life was going to be like. The future was bright and cheery, Mom and Dad were still with us at that point, and we had no idea what being an adult entailed," she says without looking at me.

"Is the future anything like what you envisioned?"

"No," she responds, surprising me just enough for me to look at her profile. "It's messier. It's harder. And it's better than we could have ever imagined. Not the answer you were expecting, huh?"

I shake my head. "No, not really. I was thinking you'd give me an answer that's more cliché."

"Why would I do that? I don't lie, especially not to people I love and call family. What's on your mind?"

Deep breath. I take three.

"I don't feel ready. Marriage, yes, I'm ready for that. We've already been doing it for a week and I'm in it for the forever part of those vows. I adore Fisher and am so happy I get to spend the rest of my life with him. It's parenting that's really making me panic these days. Dan and Julie did a good job with me considering how I started out, but what if I can't do the same for Gen and Jax? What if I screw them up the way my mother could have if I hadn't ended up in foster care? What if I hadn't ended up finally with Dan and Julie? My entire life could have turned out so different."

She laughs loudly enough to catch the attention of the tables around us.

"Do you and my brother ever talk about these things? Are you sharing a brain lately? I swear, I had this same exact conversation with him a week or so ago," she says.

Turning in her seat, Jacelyn takes my hands in hers and stares at me. Her laughter, the humor in her eyes, fades and her demeanor becomes serious. I feel my pulse kick up a notch and I'm a little fearful of what she might say next.

"You are going to be the best damn mom out there. It's not because of who raised you up or if they did it right. It's because you love with everything in you. So does Fish. These kids are so fucking lucky to have two parents who chose them," she says emphatically. She lets the words hang in the air. "You chose them. With their pasts and fear and stories about people leaving them behind. They're going to have you guys to be there when they wake up scared or when it's hard for them to explain why they react to something a certain way. You are choosing to be their parents and that is probably the greatest gift you could ever give to a child."

I'm not even sure how to respond. Should I respond? She's given the positives of Fisher and me being parents a lot of thought. I've definitely been focusing on the negatives and how I feel I might not be ready to live up to the image I have in my head of the perfect family. I was fully prepared to never have a white picket fence life. When I started my journey to adoption, I didn't even have an apartment big enough to accommodate all of us. I didn't expect a man to pop into my life and offer me space to be myself and welcome my dreams of having an unconventional family, too.

"Listen. Parenting is literally the hardest job ever. Tommy and I are just getting started, and we're getting them fresh from the oven. I cannot imagine the amount of stress you and my brother are under knowing you're about to have children who have already been kids for a long time before you get to be parents. I don't even know if that makes sense, but bear with me," she says.

Jacey scrunches up her nose like she's trying to hold back tears. If she breaks down, I can't guarantee I won't as well. The last few months have been a rollercoaster ride and I might be lying on a regular basis when I tell people I'm doing okay.

"We have been immensely fortunate in the sense that family is everything around here. There are extra grandparents and bonus aunts and uncles just a phone call or short walk away, plus a ton of amazing cousins to hang with," Jacelyn says. "My brother is one of the good ones and if he hadn't seen good in you, he wouldn't have acted like a fool. I cannot wait for the two of you to raise your babies and make our childhood home a home once again."

I nod but stay quiet for a minute longer, watching as Greg saunters up to the mic with a guitar. He looks to the back of the room where Caryn is watching from the counter while helping with coffee orders. There's a twinkle in his eyes before he begins strumming a tune I know with every fiber of my soul. Closing my eyes, I listen as the sound of Bob Marley's "Is

This Love" fills the room, and I smile because I know this is the song he picked out for Caryn tonight. They spent their honeymoon locked away in Jamaica and came home with a longing for island life. Theirs was the first actual wedding cake I made for anyone here, but that was before they were like an extension of my family.

Family.

"I am so glad I fell in love with him. I get to have all of you, too, and that's not something I ever thought I would have," I say, reaching my hand out and grasping Jacey's fingers. "Fortunate, I don't think, even begins to describe all of my emotions."

*****

He slowly removes my jacket once we step through the doorway, brushing the snow from the fabric before hanging it in the coat closet. I watch his movements intently, wondering if this was the kind of thing his father used to do for his mother. Will our children be so privileged to learn the same kind of respect and love from their father?

"They'll be here tomorrow," I say cautiously when he turns toward me after hanging his own jacket alongside mine.

His smile tells me everything I need to know. Everything is going to be just fine.

"Are you nervous?" he asks.

Their beds are made. New toothbrushes are in the bathroom for them. Jax's bookcase has a new Rick Riordan book to get him started. Gen's bookcase features Minecraft figurines. On top of their dressers is a picture of them with my mom and dad. I've stopped calling them by their actual names. It doesn't matter that they didn't raise me from the start, they got me to the end. Now, they're giving my children the chance to grow up in a home where love is the one thing we can all rely on.

"No," I say. My forehead wrinkles as I think about what I am feeling. "I'm excited. This is going to be an adventure and I can't imagine anyone I'd rather do this with than you."

I kick off my shoes and he unties his boots. We set them by the door. He takes my hand in his, turns off the kitchen light, and slowly pulls me into his arms.

"You, my Delilah, are going to be the greatest mom ever," he says quietly, then places his lips to my forehead.

I feel my body relax against his for a brief moment before we wander through the house, me following his lead toward the stairs as he takes me from one bedroom to the next. We stare at the beds knowing they soon won't be empty. We hope they'll like the new luggage sets we bought for them — not because we want them to go anywhere, but because we plan on taking them everywhere. Neither of us ever had real vacations or weekends away. I wasn't given those opportunities and Fisher's parents were so consumed with the restaurant there wasn't time.

We're going to make time. Time is all we have.

And as of tomorrow, it's all theirs.

Chapter 36

Fisher

Tommy adjusts my bowtie and I swallow hard. Again.

I can't seem to catch my breath or keep my mouth from going dry.

"Will you stop fidgeting? Damn it, Fish, you're sweating a lot. Maybe you should go stand outside for a few minutes," he says.

I'm sure standing out in the cold winter weather for five minutes would help a little, but it won't get me any closer to the moment I marry her. Again.

"Nah. I'm fine. It's all good. Everything is under control."

Tommy looks at me suspiciously, his right eyebrow rising.

"You didn't place any bets on anything did you?" He straightens the lapels on my suit roughly before laying his hands on my shoulders.

I squint my eyes and glare at him. Why on earth would he think something like that? Then I realize, my reaction to a situation that makes me nervous is to sweat like crazy and say things are "fine" and "under control." It's the same way I react when a bet doesn't go my way. My gambling hasn't been an issue in a long time, though, and I still feel indebted to him for rescuing me from myself. He pulled me out of a fire I created. He saved my life.

I relax my face and smile at him.

"I did not. That hasn't even been a thought, but I think if I still were a betting man ... I would bet my life my future wife is not freaking out about what we're about to do."

And why would she? We're already married in the eyes of the state. The "big" wedding is for the family. It's for us, too, but mostly it's for the pictures and the party and time with all our closest people.

Tommy laughs loudly and it causes heads to turn.

"I'll let you have that one bet, but it's the last one," he says, holding his fist up for me to bump.

"You got it."

He turns away from me as Jonah comes running in the room. I watch my brother-in-law lift his son into his arms and I have myself a moment. My soon-to-be son is a little big to be picking up quite that easily, but I'm here for the hugs. I'm here for all of it.

The kids have been in Brockport just a handful of days, but already it feels like they've been part of our little family right from the beginning.

When Delilah started the process of petitioning for adoption, we were hardly a thing. She knew she wanted to be a mom, and knew she wanted to provide a home to kids who maybe weren't coming from the best situations. I have never once questioned her want to adopt and we haven't discussed having biological children. Honestly, though, I'm okay either way. We're a family no matter what.

Father Murphy walks in the room, points, and motions for me to follow him. Pushing my hands into my suit pockets, I push up onto the toes of my shiny shoes and step in his direction.

When I reach him, he glances at the watch on his left hand while holding a Bible in his right.

"Are you ready?"

"Ready? Are we doing something today, Murph?"

His smile reaches his eyes. He shrugs his shoulders.

"Nothing huge. I just figured I would stand in front of a bunch of people and say some nice things about you and Delilah, have you repeat some stuff after me, and ask her twice if she's really, really sure you're the one she wants to do this life with," he says. The smile never leaves his face. "This has been my favorite wedding this year, Fish. I'm absolutely overjoyed to see you start your family. But in all seriousness, it's just about time for you to go out and wait for her."

"You know, I feel like I've been waiting for her my entire life. I didn't know how much I needed to find my person until she found me," I say, feeling the emotion bubble up in my chest.

I've been feeling a lot of feelings lately and I'm not used to it yet. Tommy told me it happens when you find the person you're meant to be with. He said it gets worse as you have kids, so I'm attempting to steel myself from the onslaught of emotions as the kids get more settled into our home.

"That's usually how it happens, Fisher," he says, his smile faltering just a bit.

I hold my hand out to shake his, he places the Bible in the crook of his left elbow and accepts the gesture. Then he surprises me as he pulls me in for a hug.

"I cannot think of a better family to take her in. It's like she was meant to find home here in our little town."

I tighten my arm around him, but let him have those last words. I can't think of a better family either.

*****

Dan gently holds his hand over hers as they slowly begin the trek from the head table to the dance floor. Delilah takes small, measured steps not because that's how it's supposed to be done, but because Dan's still healing. He's come a long way since that night in September, though, and we're all grateful he's even here at all.

When they finally reach the center of the floor, he kisses her cheek and takes her in his arms for the father-daughter dance. I hear the, "I love you," in every movement.

There were moments when we thought Dan might not be able to walk unassisted and there have been hard days for him and Julie as he tried to get through physical therapy without showing he was struggling. She pushed him, and sometimes he would push back, but in the end, we witnessed what marriage is. If Delilah and I have learned anything from watching how her parents have risen against the hardship it's how to come together as a unit in the face of adversity.

All the married friends and family in our circle have taught us the importance of talking to one another. I've seen my sister and Tommy argue about stupid things that leave her in tears and him stuck in his office. But I've also seen them grow as a couple through what they've gone through. Delilah and I know there are going to be difficult times in our marriage. We expect them to happen. But, we have so many lessons to learn from one another.

This woman, my wife, was so loved for so long and now I have the rest of my life to love her, too. I plan to make her feel that love every day as we start this adventure.

I miss the end of their dance and am still thinking about all the things we have to learn when I feel her arms wrap around from behind me. Her hands settle on my chest and I feel her ear nestle against my back. My left hand finds hers, pressing her palm more snugly against my chest and intertwining our fingers. I lift our hands and place my lips against her fingertips, kissing them one at a time.

We spend a moment quietly together in the center of the chaos our families are making as they take to the floor, bringing the party to life. As they make their way past us, Jaxson and Genevieve pull us all together.

That's when I feel it. Again. It's all the pieces we were missing. They slid into the spots they were meant to fill and created us when we weren't paying attention.

Epilogue

EIGHTEEN MONTHS LATER

Delilah

We've been parents for a grand total of twelve months.

There have been bumps and bruises and hiccups, but every single day I wake up with a grateful heart. It took longer than we hoped it would to finalize Genevieve and Jaxson's adoption, but it didn't stop us from living life at full speed with them right beside us. I think we planned to get them home and immediately they would be ours, but six months into having them with us as foster children is when all the paperwork was finally approved. In reality, we knew it would be at least that long, possibly longer, but we were crossing our fingers it would be less than that.

There's a picture of the four of us with the judge hanging in that formal dining room no one ever used once my mother- and father-in-law passed away. We use it all the time now. We have to ... there are a lot more family dinners during the week and it's the one table that fits most of us when we get together for Sunday supper with Jacey's crew. There are plenty of meals shared at the island counter in the kitchen, but Fisher and I also know the big table one room over should be used for more than just fancy meals.

My parents have moved closer to us, which is a huge blessing. When they made the decision to no longer be foster parents once Gen and Jax came home to us, they put the house up for sale and made the move to Brockport. Fortunately for us, there was a Cape Cod style home just down the road that was small enough for them. It's also large enough for the kids to spend the night when they want to, which hasn't happened yet. Someday we'll take advantage of Mom and Dad being so close and plan a weekend away without Gen and Jax, but we aren't in any rush.

In the last eighteen months, we've celebrated three birthdays — Genevieve is 13 now and Jax is 10. Fisher and I agree that it hurts to not have met them sooner, but we're taking every day as a way to make up for the time we feel we lost. We know it was meant to happen the way it did. I couldn't have these kids without having Fisher, too, and he couldn't have me without the kids.

Life would never be right if it had happened a different way.

"Mom, are we putting the cupcakes in the display a certain way?" she asks. Genevieve looks at the cupcake trays on the counter and laughs. "I'm pretty sure you did every color of the rainbow."

My heart smiles hearing her call me "mom" and I will never tire of the name.

"It's the first day of June," I say.

Her face lights up.

"Pride. I should have known you planned this. You plan for every holiday."

I watch my daughter pop an earbud back in and get to work arranging cupcakes. One red, two orange, three yellow, and so on until the top row of the case is filled and she kneels down to begin on the second row. I'm planning for a big cupcake sale day.

"So, I was thinking," Maggie says as she comes out of the kitchen, "that we should offer cake decorating classes. And by we I mean you and I can assist because I'm a bitchin' assistant."

I clear my throat, knowing she's oblivious to the fact Genevieve is crouched down behind the display case. She winces when she figures it out.

"Sorry kid!" she yells.

Gen laughs loudly.

"It's fine, Aunt Maggie. I've heard way worse. Did you forget I go to public school?"

Maggie rolls her eyes dramatically.

"No, missy. I did not forget. Just make sure when you use the words you're learning they're in proper context, m'kay?"

"Yes, ma'am," she says, saluting Maggie as she crouches back down to finish filling the display.

I look at Maggie expectantly, waiting for her to continue her thought about classes.

"So, this cake decorating class …" Genevieve says quietly while she works.

Her voice trails off and leaves me wanting more from her.

"Yes?" I say to urge her on.

Use your voice, baby. Tell me what you want, I say silently. We've been working with the kids to speak up when they want to ask a question. I've specifically encouraged Gen to climb out of the box she's slowly been putting herself into since moving to the country. The adjustment to the occasional small-minded asshole has been difficult for her outspoken New York City attitude, to say the least. She's rented space inside her head to people who won't matter five years from now. I don't want her to change who she is to suit people who wouldn't even love her if she was perfect by their standards.

I watch as she pulls herself to standing behind the display case and leans against the glass, crossing her arms and looking deep into my heart.

"Do you think it would be open to people of all ages, or just adults? I've been watching as you work and I think I can do it. You've let me practice a few things, but I want to learn for real," she says. Biting her lip and thinking hard, she finally asks, "Will you let me take the class?"

Maggie and I exchange a glance, a smile, perhaps it's even a knowing look. We both see talent when we give Gen control of a project.

"What if we make it a themed class?" Mags says. "We could do some geared toward adults and some toward kids. Petals and lace for one week, Minecraft Creepers on another? But, if your mom is okay with it, I don't see why we shouldn't have them open to anyone who wants to learn."

Genevieve's eyes light up. She's not so much into Minecraft these days, but her brother is and his birthday is on the horizon. She's already sketched out a few ideas she was working on for me to create, but if she wants me to help her with a cake for Jax, I would happily step aside and let her take the reins.

I step behind the counter and fiddle with the buttons on the bakery's audio system until the music comes to life. We're still getting used to the space. Like other things in my life, making the dream of owning a bakery a reality took longer than expected. A little more than a year after I originally started looking at spaces, we closed on a storefront just down the street from The Jumping Bean. It took a lot of work, but after tearing down walls and recreating the interior the way I wanted it, we opened in April.

We haven't had a day without a steady stream of patrons since.

"It's time to open," I say. "Let's unlock the shop and then we'll get to brainstorming these themed decorating classes."

Maggie and Genevieve reach for pens and paper as I walk to the door and flip the lock.

I am in love with my life.

It's taken me a while to appreciate where I came from. Watching my daughter fall in love with her childhood, though, has made every failed attempt to hide myself away worth it. I tried for a long time to shrink into a box small enough to keep me out of someone else's spotlight, but it didn't work. I was born to stand out, and so was she.

Fisher

If you had said to me a couple years ago, "Fisher, you're going to be married to an awesome woman, have two freaking awesome kids, and a thriving business two years from now," I would have laughed right in your face. That was the me who didn't think I deserved this kind of happiness. That's the me who was still camped out in the delusion that all my wrongs weren't worth receiving grace from others.

Now? I am a dad. She is a mom. We are a family. And the truth is, we all deserve to be happy.

It's no secret I almost screwed up any chance I had to be with Delilah, and that was before we even knew each other's names. Thankfully, I had family who pushed me to apologize. I can't imagine how lonely I would be at this point in my life if I hadn't sent her flowers and a stand mixer. I can't wrap my mind around how quiet my house would be without my children's laughter or music playing in the kitchen while my wife bakes her heart out.

"Will you pass the forks, please?"

I look up from the counter where I'm mixing together a rub for pulled pork. My thoughts drift a lot lately.

"Huh?" I ask, having missed the question entirely.

"You're in your head again, Daddy. I need the forks. I ran out and need to finish wrapping the silverware," Jax says, pointing to a bin filled with plastic forks.

We have an event to cater this weekend and he's become my designated flatware wrapper. He's actually been doing it for every event we've been hired to serve at since the day he and Genevieve came to live with us. One evening I was rolling silverware at the dining room table to get ahead for the next event when Jax sat down and started talking. But, he fidgets, so handing him a stack of napkins and sliding the silverware between us pulled the moment together. That's how we've learned about one another.

"You know," I say, picking up the bin and handing it to him, "I used to do this job when I was your age. Not for catered things, because we didn't cater things back then, but for the restaurant."

"Did you like doing it?" he asks while grabbing one of each piece of flatware and setting them on a napkin to roll together.

Using a fork to combine my ingredients, I pull my bottom lip in between my teeth. The funny thing is, Genevieve makes the same face when she's mulling something over. Delilah calls it our thinking face. I've been thinking a lot the last eighteen months — about parenting, my parents, fostering, adopting, the restaurant. So many things to think about.

"I didn't love it, but it was something to do with my dad. The restaurant was our life and I'm glad I was able to be here to work with Pop on all the little details. I learned a lot," I say, looking down into the bowl of spices and feeling the emotion flood over me.

"That's kind of how I feel about it, too," Jax says, shrugging. "Except, you don't make the restaurant your whole life. We do a lot of fun stuff, too."

We share a smile and I nod.

"Yeah, we certainly do, don't we?"

Work isn't my number one priority anymore. I still spend more time than I need to at the restaurant, but I'm learning to let others help. As the catering side of the business started to take off, I added additional staff to help with the administrative duties. My heart is in the cooking, not the books, so I get to focus on what I do love and my family. Plus, Delilah and I force each other to take days off. We know others can manage things for a couple days if we want to have family time.

Wedding season is just starting, so Delilah and I are both booked pretty solid for the next few months, but that's not going to stop us from letting the kids be kids. Evelyn has an equestrian camp in July that Jaxson was interested in and, he doesn't know, but we signed him up as a birthday gift. Genevieve has been tapping into her artistic side when at the bakery with her mom, so she'll also be spending time with Jacelyn at the studio doing some art camps and events.

And what are Delilah and I going to do while they're off creating memories?

Who knows? I guess that's for us to figure out.

One thing I am certain of — we're going to make good use of the time we have together. Whether it's hanging out with our kids and listening to all the stories they have from their time away from each other or just the two of us curled up on the couch, we're going to keep living like we're famous in a small town.

The end ... for now.

Acknowledgments

This book … oof. The story came easy. The rest of it? Not so much. It sat on my hard drive for more than a year after it was done, untouched, fully edited, read through by someone for the sensitive content surrounding foster care, and I just couldn't. The ability to take the next step wasn't there.

I started writing Fisher and Delilah's story on April 1, 2019. At the time, I was newly pregnant with Sammy, our surprise, and still dealing with some major depression and anxiety after finishing Letters from Emily and attempting to write Caryn and Greg's book, which was then indefinitely put on hold. I may revisit them in the future; they need to grow first. By the time I was done writing, Sammy was close to celebrating his second birthday, we added a puppy to the insanity, COVID had knocked all normal out of our lives, and at least one of my kids had achieved the rank of Black Belt with another continuing to prepare for the same.

You would think I would have gotten all the details hammered out, table of contents created, even a cover for this book as soon as the writing was done. I was frozen and couldn't bring myself to do any of it. Instead of doing all the little things to get this one ready for you, I started writing a second and third book in this new series.

You see, I'm not ready to leave Brockport behind. I am too attached to the characters who started this adventure to let them not pop up once in a while. So, yes, the entire family makes appearances, but as you can see there are new friends and found family I hope you will fall in love with the way you did back when you met Brian and Stella and their entire crew.

It's time to move forward.

The Dunkin Drive-Thru employees, Yogi Tea, and protein shakes: You are a blessing.

My readers: There are a lot of emotions. Thank you for sticking with me through this, for finding me and encouraging me in the midst of not publishing new material, and continuing to stand by me. I know it's easy to forget the little authors when there are so many amazing writers out there producing a never-ending backlist of titles, so if you've stuck with me I hope you know how much you mean to me. I love you all.

Sean Burns: Thank you for sitting with me on the deck in the Outer Banks as I talked through some of the difficult plot holes I was trying to manage in August 2021. At the time I'm writing this, you're the only one who has read this book from start to finish and I cannot love you enough for letting me share this story with you first.

Taylor Delong and Marissa Frosch: I wouldn't be at the point of actually writing this page if it wasn't for your support, encouragement, and authorly love. Thank you for poking me when I need it and commiserating about life in general when there's a plot twist. It's time to manifest good shit, my dudes.

Carrie, Vicci, Bridgett, Sandi, Liz, Melissa, Beth, Sarah, Ebony, Jen: Thank you a million times for offering to beta read Fisher and Delilah's story. Your attention to detail and feedback were so important to this whole process. It means the world to me to have you as part of my book family.

Shihan Theron Feidt: Thank you for having a space at the dojo for parents like me who need to get things done but have a crazy kid activity schedule. A majority of this book happened while standing at the counter and sitting in my car at team runs watching my kids become Black Belts. I appreciate everything you've done for my family, but especially for allowing me a place to breathe when things get hard.

And finally, my family: I love you and our insane life, but will you please let me work a little more? Boy Wonder, I cannot thank you enough for taking the initiative to put a locking doorknob on the basement so I can hide away, pop in my ear buds, and attempt to ignore the sounds of WWE Smack Down in the front room directly above my head. Don't forget to switch the laundry and start the dishwasher.

About the Author

M.L. Pennock is a former journalist turned author. She attended Alfred University, earning a Bachelor of Arts in English and communication studies, before going on to earn a Master of Arts in communications from SUNY College at Brockport. She lives in Central New York with her husband, four children, and Siberian Husky, Tikaani.

M.L. Pennock is the author of the To Have series.

Visit facebook.com/mlpennock or mlpennock.com for more information about what she's working on next.